3.95

This b... ...le be

SCHOOL

# ELLIOTT
# & WIN

# ELLIOTT
# & WIN

## Carolyn Meyer

Collier Books
Macmillan Publishing Company
New York

First Collier Books edition 1990

Collier Books
Macmillan Publishing Company
866 Third Avenue, New York, NY 10022
Collier Macmillan Canada, Inc.

Printed in the United States of America

A hardcover edition of *Elliott & Win* is available from Margaret
K. McElderry Books, Macmillan Publishing Company.

10 9 8 7 6 5 4 3 2 1

Library of Congress Cataloging-in-Publication Data

Meyer, Carolyn
Elliott & Win/Carolyn Meyer. — 1st Collier Books ed.    p.         cm.
Summary: Fourteen-year-old Win hopes to receive support and
guidance in self-acceptance from his adult friend Elliott, despite
another boy's insistence that Elliott is homosexual.
ISBN 0-02-044702-7
[1. Sex role — Fiction. 2. Self-acceptance — Fiction.] I. Title.
II. Title: Elliott and Win. PZ7.M5685E1     1990     [Fic] — dc20     89-70868 CI

TO MY FRIEND GEORGE

# CONTENTS

# ELLIOTT
# & WIN

# ONE

---

# DOUBLE NEGATIVES

"**W**HERE's the TV?"

I had checked out every inch of the place, taking my time. Unless it was hidden by a secret door or concealed like a wall safe behind a painting, there was no television in that house.

"Sorry, Winston, I don't own one," Elliott called from the kitchen and kept on doing whatever he was doing out there.

No TV, but a stereo set that must have cost a pile of bills. Shelves packed with records, tapes and books climbed all the way to the ceiling. Where there weren't shelves, there were pictures: wild-colored paintings of blobby shapes, drawings of dead ducks and apples and photographs, mostly of doors. Why would anybody take a picture of a door? When I asked Elliott why doors, he said, "I was attempting to capture the texture and the play of light and shadow."

A big white sofa fenced in three sides of a glass table standing on a square of black and red carpet. On the table was a thing made of twisted aluminum tubes that looked like a piece of a wrecked car and a nice piece of wood that had been hacked and gouged and then polished. If you didn't feel like staring at them you could look out huge windows at the mountains. Next to the fireplace was a black leather chair with a lamp and a table stacked with books and magazines. Elliott's throne.

When something grabbed my attention, I'd holler, "Hey, Elliott, where did you get *this*?" and Elliott would come in wearing his long striped apron, carrying a knife or a wooden spoon, and tell me— Alaska, Russia, Peru, and other such places—and explain what the thing was.

My exploration of Elliott's place continued until I headed into the dining room and almost ran dead into a life-size stuffed figure of a fat lady with a bandanna around her head. She was dressed in a regular blue dress, slant-eyed glasses on her nose and a dustrag in her apron pocket, and she leaned on a broom. She looked so real I let out a squawk.

"You must have met Conchita," Elliott said from the kitchen. "She creates quite an effect, doesn't she?"

I edged past Conchita and went to see what Elliott was up to.

The kitchen was almost as amazing as the rest I'd seen of the house. A gigantic wooden block stood on chubby legs in the center of the room with racks of knives like guns in holsters. Copper pots dangled from hooks above the block. Elliott was pouring oil into a blender drop by drop.

"You got a Cuisinart?"

"I wouldn't have one," Elliott said.

"How come? Ma keeps saying she wants a food processor, but Donny and me told her a bigger can opener would probably do it. Ma hates to cook."

"Personally I prefer to handle the food myself. I don't buy gadgets, just good basic tools. The blender is an exception."

I leaned on the counter next to Elliott and watched him. I felt like a midget next to Elliott, who was at least six foot two. "What's that stuff you're making?"

"Mayonnaise."

I couldn't help it; I laughed. Who ever heard of making mayonnaise when you could buy it in a jar? "What for?"

"For the chicken salad."

"Chicken *salad*? That's what we're having?"

"Among other things. I have some gazpacho left from last night, and the bread I baked this morning."

The bread better be good; I didn't like salads or anything green, and the other stuff, whatever it was, sounded like a bad idea. I'd been hoping we'd go to Burger Shed.

Elliott asked if I minded eating in the kitchen, and I told him I didn't. Without TV it didn't make much difference where we ate. At home we had supper off trays and watched whatever was on television, which suited me fine because then I didn't have to talk much.

Elliott had set the little table by the window with woven placemats and real napkins that matched. He cut slices of bread from a grainy brown loaf on a board

and put bowls of something like chopped-up tomatoes
at each place. I hated tomatoes.

"Gazpacho," said Elliott, when he saw me staring. "It's a cold Spanish soup, although I've heard it
described as a liquid salad."

In the middle of the table he set the plate of
chicken mixed with his special mayo and decorated
with pieces of black olive and red pepper. He poured
white wine into a goblet with a long, thin stem.

"What can I get for you, Winston?" Elliott asked.
"I have mineral water and iced tea, and I think there's
some kefir if you'd prefer that."

"You got any Dr Pepper?"

"No. I never buy soft drinks," he said, twisting up
his mouth to show that soda was in the same category
as television. "But I suppose when you come here
again, I could have some."

"Iced tea is okay." No television. No soda. I
hoped at least there'd be sugar for the iced tea. There
was, and a long silver spoon to stir it with.

"Three spoons of sugar, Winston?" he said,
watching me. "You do like it sweet, don't you?"

"Yeah."

"Well, then, *salud,*" Elliott said, lifting his wine-
glass and clicking against my iced tea, and I said,
"Salute," as though I had meals served like this every
day. I tasted a spoonful of the chopped-up tomatoes,
which turned out to be even worse than I expected.

"How do you like the gazpacho?"

"It's, uh, fine. You always make this kind of
stuff?"

"Most of the time. I like to eat well, and therefore,
since I'm a bachelor, I had to learn to cook well."

Ma had lectured me for two days on how I had to be polite to Mr. Deerfield, so I forced down more cold soup.

"Well, Winston," Elliott said, putting the bowls in the sink, his empty, mine full, "I hope you find the rest of our meal more to your liking."

I did too, but I wasn't counting on it and didn't know what to say. I said, "Would you please call me Win? I don't like to be called Winston."

"I *see*," Elliott said. He passed the board with the bread on it and a dish with a china cow's head covering a lump of butter. "But it's a very distinguished name. Were you called after someone? Winston Churchill, for instance? Or is it a family name?"

I took two big slices of bread and a tiny scoop of chicken salad from the plate, hoping I could scrounge some leftovers at home. "Neither one. I was named for the cigarette."

Elliott seemed to choke. "The cigarette?"

"My dad was trying to quit smoking when I was born, and I guess he was really dying for some nicotine." I never knew whether to believe this story or not, but it's what I had been told. "You know that ad, 'Winston tastes good like a cigarette should'?"

"A regrettably ungrammatical expression," Elliott said in a teachery voice. "The correct way to say it is, 'Winston tastes good *as* a cigarette should.' *As*, not *like*."

"I don't see what difference it makes." I was carefully picking off the pieces of olive and pepper, which I didn't like any more than I liked conversations about grammar.

"I suppose it doesn't to some people. But good

language is as important to me as good food or good art. I wouldn't use bad grammar any more than I would eat a TV dinner or hang a piece of trash on my walls." He poured more wine out of the bottle with a French label. "This is really an excellent chenin blanc," he said, more or less to himself.

I had to get a crazy one, I thought, poking at the chicken salad, which had a strange fishy taste. It was Ma's fault. She thought I needed to have an adult male in my life. She came to the conclusion after Joe Favello had left and we moved down from Colorado to New Mexico; that was only a few weeks earlier. Joe was not my father; my father was Michael X. Kelly, who was two before Joe. First Michael, then Bobby Don Willett, then Joe, now nobody.

Ma said never again, she'd had it with men, they came into your life and made you fall in love and then they turned around and left you. You could not trust any of them. "Are all men like that?" I asked her, and she said maybe not, but she was too tired to go looking for the exception to the rule.

But, Ma said, if my little brother Donny and I were to grow up to amount to anything, we ought to have a man around, somebody to do things with every week or so and be what she called a "good influence." This made no sense to me, because we'd just turn out to be like all those other men, wouldn't we?

It was useless to argue with Ma. She signed us up with Los Amigos, because Paul Crowser's mother had done that. DeeDee Crowser was Ma's friend, and the two of them got together and decided this would be good for their sons. Los Amigos was an organization that took boys like Paul and Donny and me who didn't see our fathers much and matched us up with men like Elliott Deerfield who volunteered to help. The booklet the social worker gave Ma talked about "being a role model" and "giving the precious gift of friendship." Donny hadn't been given an amigo yet.

Paul had been in the program for six months. His amigo, Vinny Baca, drove a potato chip truck and had a wife and four little girls. He and Paul went bowling and saw ball games and horror movies, which the girls were too young for. Vinny's wife fixed them enchiladas and tamales, and they had soda and ice cream and other normal food. If Mrs. Baca ever fixed liquid salad, Paul never mentioned it.

But I got matched up with a man who didn't own a TV, made mayonnaise and lived in a museum with a stuffed cleaning lady. I never was the luckiest person in the world, and that's what got me paired with a basically weird person. It was not forever, the social worker at Los Amigos told me. Elliott and I were on a trial basis for six weeks. If we got along well, we'd be amigos for at least a year, maybe more. But if it didn't work out, at the end of six weeks either one of us could say so and we'd each be assigned a new amigo. There was still the chance that I would get somebody like Vinny Baca, or at least somebody who *ate* like Vinny Baca, and another amigo would be found for Elliott.

"How's the chicken salad?"

I was still shoving it around the plate. Ma made me promise I'd eat whatever was served, but I thought we'd go to a restaurant and I could order whatever I wanted. I downed the salad in a couple of big bites, so I wouldn't have to taste it.

"Uh. It's real good."

"Would you like some more?"

"No, I don't want no more."

With that Elliott dumped a fat spoonful of the stuff on my plate. Hey, I thought, can't he hear? So I said clearly, "I don't want no more, *thank you*." And Elliott laid another pile next to the first one. "Cut it out!" I said and pushed his hand away, because it looked as though Elliott was going to bomb me again. "What'd you do that for?"

"You said, I believe, 'I don't want no more.'"

"Yeah, right. So?"

"That's a double negative. If you *don't* want *no* more, then that must mean you *do* want some more."

Elliott pulled a yellow pad and a pen out of a drawer behind his chair and began writing. He shoved the pad across the table toward me.

I DO NOT WANT NO MORE.

"The two negatives, *not* and *no*, cancel each other out." He reached over and drew lines through not and no. "There. Now read it."

"'I do want more.' Okay, I get it," I said, dimly remembering something Mrs. Metcalfe, my Language Arts teacher, had put us through. I really hated grammar. I didn't see any point to memorizing all that stuff. People like Elliott and Mrs. Metcalfe were the only ones who cared.

"So how do you say it if you *don't* want more?"

"I don't want any more, thank you," I mumbled, but Elliott smiled as though I had just said something highly intelligent.

"You don't need to eat what I put on your plate," Elliott said. "I was merely trying to illustrate a point."

But I felt bad about not liking the soup or the

chicken, because Elliott had gone to a lot of trouble for me and I wanted to do something right. So I ate it. Every mouthful.

After such a gourmet dinner, I was expecting a gourmet dessert—something in flames, maybe. Instead Elliott brought out a bowl of nuts in their shells and a chunk of dried-up cheese.

"Fresh parmesan," he explained, handing me a nutcracker. "There's absolutely nothing like it with walnuts."

And that was Elliott Deerfield's idea of dessert. Six weeks of *this*?

# TWO

# THE FUTURE OF AMERICA

"**I**'M GOING to have coffee and a little brandy in the living room," Elliott announced. "Would you like some more iced tea?" He poured coffee thick as mud into a tiny cup and dark gold-colored stuff into a little glass that looked as though it had been cut from a diamond. "Crystal," he said before I could ask him, "from Ireland." That got my attention, because Michael X. Kelly is Irish, and therefore so am I.

Elliott had munched down those walnuts and cheese with the same look Donny got over M&M's, while I made a mess with the shells. Now he put the cup and glass on the table next to his throne and set the iced tea on the coffee table. He turned on the stereo and excused himself to go to the bathroom. As soon as he was gone, I flopped into his leather chair.

The chair was on a swivel, and it had a lever on the side to lock it at an angle if you leaned back. I fooled around with it, tipping and swiveling. When I heard the toilet flush I gave the chair another twirl, whacking the table with my knee as I spun by. I saw the crystal glass sail up, the brandy fly out and splash on the rug, and I heard a sickening clink. Elliott came out of the bathroom as I pried myself out of the tipped-back chair, the beautiful Irish glass lying on the floor in pieces, the brandy soaking into the rug.

"I'm sorry," I said, feeling my face go red and hot, waiting for Elliott to get furious.

But all he said was, "I'll get a sponge."

The glass had broken into three neat pieces. "Maybe it could be fixed."

"No, but it doesn't matter. Win, I don't want you to be upset about this. It's only a glass. That's not the worst thing that could happen."

But I felt bad, worse than I did about not liking the food, and I didn't know what to do. "Could I take the pieces home?"

"Certainly." We wrapped them in paper napkins, which I stuffed in the pockets of my jeans.

Elliott poured himself another brandy in a different kind of glass and settled into his chair. I sat up on the edge of the white sofa as though it were a hot stove. Every time Elliott took a sip of brandy, I took a sip of tea, being careful to put the glass down on the coaster. The stereo was still playing, and Elliott began waving his hand like a conductor. An opera, he explained, mentioning what it was and who wrote it, which I forgot as soon as I heard it. Then Elliott began asking questions about my family.

I told him about Ma cleaning houses, not for just anybody but for people like a famous Hollywood actress and a bigshot from Washington, D.C. Once a week she picked up a stack of abused jeans from DenimWerx and brought them home and patched them on her old sewing machine. She got paid by the patch. What she really liked was embroidery. I described the jacket she had made for Bobby Don, embroidered all over with unicorns. A writer came to town and photographed the jacket and promised to send the book he was writing about present-day folk art. He never sent it. Ma saw it one day in a bookstore, and there was the unicorn jacket, right on the cover, in color. She bought the book herself.

On weekends Ma played the guitar at a restaurant, and two nights a week she went to school to learn word processing. She liked to clean houses and sew, because she said you could think whatever you wanted to think while you were doing it. After she graduated she would quit her other jobs and go to work in an office and make more money, but then she'd have to think about nothing but word processing. I thought it sounded boring.

We hadn't lived in Santa Fe very long. We were in Durango, Colorado, for five years, but there wasn't much work in that little town. Then DeeDee Crowser, who used to be our next-door neighbor, wrote to Ma and said it was better in Santa Fe. Ma asked me if I cared if we moved. I said I didn't, but could we go to Denver or at least Albuquerque? But Ma didn't like big cities; she said they destroyed her spirit. As soon as school was out, we packed everything into a rented truck and drove to Santa Fe, because Ma thought she could get a job with a company that processed film. That didn't work out, and there was no money to go back to Durango. Ma said we just had to make the best of it, and she took whatever she could find.

Donny was seven, I told Elliott, born when Ma was married to Bobby Don. Donny slept in the same bed with me which was awful, because Donny often had bad dreams and thrashed around and sometimes wet the bed.

"And what about your father?"

I hated that question, because there wasn't any answer. "I haven't seen him for a long time. Not for seven years. He used to write sometimes. He's a trucker. He has a new wife and family in California. Ma says it's what happens and there's no point thinking about it."

But I did think about it. I pictured myself getting a motorcycle, a Yamaha like Joe Favello's with the windjammer fairing wrapped around the handlebars, and riding all the way to San Diego where Michael X. Kelly lived. I still had the letter he wrote saying some day he'd take me to the zoo and to the beach and out fishing. I had never done any of those things. I dreamed of finding my father, new family or not, and saying, "Do you know who I am? I'm your son, Win Kelly." And my father would hug me the way he used to a long time ago and say "Winston-tastes-good-like-a-cigarette-should Kelly! I'm glad you're here, son."

But I didn't tell Elliott that dream. I didn't tell anybody that dream.

Elliott seemed to be listening hard. Then he asked, "What are your plans for the future?"

Another question I didn't like. I hardly ever

thought about anything past earning enough money to buy the bike and go to San Diego. When I tried to think of what Winston Allen Kelly would be doing in ten years, I couldn't. Except for one crazy idea that kept creeping into my head: *I want to be a writer.* Totally insane. My grammar (as Elliott had just pointed out) was bad, my spelling was awful, and Mrs. Metcalfe said I didn't know a comma from a hole in the ground, which made no sense—but a lot of what Mrs. Metcalfe said didn't. I wanted to write about brave people who had interesting adventures. Sometimes I started to write stories in a secret notebook, but after a couple of pages I always quit because it got too hard and the story didn't seem any good any more. Being a writer was just another dream I didn't think was worth telling Elliott.

"When I'm old enough I'm going to get a part-time job and save up to buy a motorcycle and ride out to the Coast," I said.

Elliott frowned and went to the kitchen for more coffee. Then he sank into his leather throne again and began to tell about growing up in Baltimore where his father operated a popcorn stand during the Depression. Sometimes all they had to eat for days at a time was popcorn. "To this day," Elliott said, "I can't bear to eat popcorn, or to smell it at the movies. It makes me violently ill."

I leaned back on the sofa and began to relax. "You ever been married?" The question sort of floated into my head and directly out of my mouth.

"No."

"Why not?" Maybe he felt about women the way Ma felt about men.

Elliott looked uncomfortable, as though he had just gotten a whiff of popcorn. "I see no point in marriage unless one intends to have children, and I made up my mind while I was still a youngster that I would never have any," he said, sounding like not having a wife was a matter of principle, like not having a food processor or a TV. "My parents had five children, and we were always scrambling to survive, even though my father had a fairly good job before the popcorn days. As I grew older, I got used to having everything just the way I like it. You might say I'm rather selfish."

This made me wonder why Elliott wanted to be an amigo to a kid like me. So I asked him that, too.

"Because I believe the future of America is in the hands of its youth," he said, switching to his "good food equals good grammar" voice. "People like you, Win. Quite frankly, I'm worried about the way this country is going. I want to have a hand in shaping that future. Friends of mine told me about Los Amigos. Philip and Sara Vogel are both psychologists, and she's on the board of Los Amigos. She said she was tired of hearing me moan and challenged me to *do* something. You'll meet the Vogels. Delightful people."

I wasn't sure how I felt about being shaped for the future of America. It would have been better, I thought, if Elliott said he just liked kids.

"You haven't told me what kinds of things you like to do." Elliott pulled another yellow pad out of a pile of magazines. He must have them everywhere. He put on a pair of black-rimmed half-glasses and peered at me over the tops, eyebrows raised like new moons.

My mind went blank. I couldn't think of one

thing. "Baseball games?" I said at last, even though I didn't care much about baseball.

Elliott made a face. "Baseball," he said sourly. "I will never understand why Americans have chosen that as their national sport. It's about as exciting as watching lettuce wilt. First of all, I don't like spectator sports —sitting and watching somebody else do something," he said, warming up. "Baseball and television, the two most passive activities in the world, and that's how Americans occupy their time."

I got the point: We would not be going to ball games.

"Aren't you an American?"

"Of course I'm an American. A live American, rather than a dead one, however. Now let's get some other things on this list. It doesn't have to be a *big* thing, Win."

There are a couple of movies I wouldn't have minded seeing, but I decided not to mention them. Elliott probably didn't like bowling if he didn't like baseball. I didn't bother to bring up the rock concert in Albuquerque.

"I've got some suggestions, then," Elliott said, tossing aside his glasses. "Now of course, if you don't want to do any of this, I won't try to talk you into it, and I don't want you to do it just to please me. But I do have a real treat in store for us. I've got a ticket for you for the opera!"

"The *opera?*" I was up on the edge of the sofa again.

"Have you ever seen one?"

"No." And would rather do almost anything else.

"I believe you'll find it absolutely fascinating. It's

not just the magnificent music, Win, it's the drama and the spectacle. *The Magic Flute*, of course. Wait till the Queen of the Night makes her appearance! It's still a month away, but it's not too soon to start preparing."

"What opera did you say it was?" My mind was racing in circles, trying to find a way out.

"*The Magic Flute*. Mozart. That's what we've been listening to. I'm playing it so you'll have a chance to become familiar with the music. And then of course we should go over the synopsis. The plot's tricky to follow if you're not familiar with it, especially since it's sung in Italian."

I thought the music was awful, I didn't want to listen to it or read about it, and I definitely didn't want to go. I grabbed at a wild hope: "Everybody dresses up for the opera, right? I don't have no good clothes."

Elliott sighed. "You just committed another double negative, Win. 'I don't have no good clothes' means you *do* have good clothes, which isn't what I think you intended to say. But that doesn't matter. A nice shirt will be fine. You won't feel self-conscious, I promise you."

No. No to all of this. I'd get Ma to call Los Amigos and tell them I was quitting. Elliott would try to drag me to the opera, would feed me strange foreign food, but wouldn't take me to baseball games or horror movies or let me watch TV or eat burgers and fries, all because Elliott Deerfield wanted to shape the future of America. Elliott was not what I wanted for an amigo, and I was pretty sure I wasn't what Elliott wanted either—even if he hadn't figured that out yet.

# THREE

## SGT. CROWSER

**P**AUL CROWSER pulled a little notebook and a pencil stub out of one of his pockets and began the debriefing. "Give me the story on Elliott Deerfield," he ordered.

Paul had lived next door to us in Colorado—he and his mother and his sister Vanessa who had a bleached-out punk haircut and blood-red fingernails like ten lethal weapons. I was fourteen that summer in Santa Fe; Paul was eleven months younger and small for his age. The timing of our birthdays—mine in January, his in December—put us in the same grade.

He idolized his Uncle Walter whose leg had been blown off in Vietnam and replaced with an artificial one made of green plastic. Paul dressed in camouflage shirts and pants and an ammo belt from the surplus store, and he had bummed a ragged khaki jacket with sergeant's stripes from his uncle. Paul always looked as though he was ready for battle or had just come back from one—a battle he lost.

Paul pitched a moldy canvas tent in his backyard and slept there when the weather was warm. He would have lived on field rations if his mother let him. He loved to play war. His chief topic of conversation was war. He read war books and pestered Vinny to take him to war movies. He had seen *Patton* eight times and thought of the characters in M*A*S*H as personal buddies. He behaved like an army sergeant, especially around me. It got pretty boring, but so far Paul was the only friend I had in New Mexico. The neighborhood we lived in was mostly Hispanic, which was not easy for a red-headed Anglo like me or a runty loudmouth like Paul.

Halfway between Paul's place and ours, a cinder-block shed stood in the middle of a vacant lot littered with broken bottles and rusty cans. It was windowless and dark and it smelled musty, but when Paul and I had things to talk about, that's where we went. We called it the blockhouse; Paul thought of it as his head-quarters. Nobody knew what it was really for or who owned it. Ma wouldn't let me go there at night, because she figured it was a logical place for druggies and derelicts to hang out.

When we met there, Paul brought a plastic bucket, a candle stub and matches, "rations" (usually Ritz crackers and peanut butter), and whatever else he thought we needed in the way of supplies. He turned the bucket upside down for a table, lit the candle, sat down on a cinderblock, and motioned for me to sit, too. I was prepared to answer his questions.

"Okay, he's *real* tall, and—"

"*How* tall? Be specific, Kelly."

"I don't know. More than six feet, anyhow. And he's got gray hair—"

"There's no such thing as gray hair. It only *looks* gray. It's just a bunch of white hairs mixed in with the normal colored ones."

Paul's mother was a beautician, so there was no arguing with that. And as long as we stayed with how tall Elliott was and how many white hairs he had, I was on safe ground. "His hair is a mixture of brown hairs and white hairs, and it's wavy and goes back in a V from his forehead, like this. He's a long way from being all white, though, or bald," I added, not wanting Paul to think Elliott was a decrepit old man.

"Running to fat? Getting porky?" Paul made motions with his hands for a huge potbelly.

"No. Not fat, not skinny, just big. He jumps rope."

"Jumps *rope*?"

"Fifteen minutes a day. He says it's all you need to do to keep in shape. He does some other things, too."

"Any distinguishing features? Scars? Warts?"

"A beard, but just on his chin. No mustache. Glasses when he reads. You know those half things that you look over the top of?"

Paul nodded and scratched something in the notebook. "What about his clothes?"

"Tan pants, short sleeved dark blue shirt—"

"Knit shirt with an alligator?"

"That's the kind, but no alligator. Plain. And a blue bandanna tied around his neck, like a scarf."

Paul frowned and I was instantly on the alert; maybe I shouldn't have mentioned the bandanna. "Shoes?"

"Deck shoes."

"With or without socks?"

I could not believe this. Who *cared*? "With."

"That's good. Jewelry?"

"Yeah. A chrome watch with all kinds of knobs and dials. An Indian silver bracelet with turquoise in it. A big hunk of turquoise in a silver ring, too."

"Which finger?"

"I don't remember."

"*Index* finger, for instance? You'd remember that."

"Ring finger, right hand." I made that up. I really couldn't remember.

"Anything else? Hat? Baseball cap or Stetson?"

"He wasn't wearing a hat. We were inside."

"But you went out to eat."

"No. We ate at his house."

"Okay, then let's get on to his wife. Describe her."

"He doesn't have a wife." Careful now, I thought; go slow. "It's just that he likes to cook, see, so he fixed some stuff and we ate there."

"No wife?"

"He's a confirmed bachelor."

"I *see*." I let out my breath when Paul switched direction and asked, "Make of car?"

"Cordova. Brown. He says he has to drive a big car because he's so big. He'd buy a Volkswagen, he says, if he could fit inside it." It was funny, picturing that big man inside a tiny car. "And he has a Land

Cruiser, too, for trips to the mountains." I liked the sound of that. Maybe this was going to come off better than I expected.

Paul seemed impressed, too. "Good," he said. "What about his house? What's it like?"

"Well, the guy's got bucks, that's for sure. He's traveled all over the world and bought rugs and artwork. For instance he has a stuffed maid—"

"A stuffed *maid?*"

"Not really, he calls it soft sculpture, but for a second I thought she was real. Her name is Conchita, and he keeps her in the dining room. You should see his stereo! Man, what I wouldn't give for a setup like that." I didn't mention the kind of records. "It's a pretty big place, too."

"How big?"

"Two bedrooms downstairs, plus a big upstairs room that he uses for an office. You go up a circular stairway, and it's got windows all around. He's got a telescope up there, too."

"Spying on the neighbors?"

"Looking at the stars." He was really crazy, Paul was. "Next to his bedroom he's got a greenhouse with a hot tub. We ate in the kitchen. In the middle of it there's one of those whatsanames, a huge block of wood for cutting things on?"

"Butcher block," Paul said.

"Yeah, that's it." Paul seemed to know everything.

"So what did you eat?"

I was ready. "Tomato soup, chicken, bread, and cheesecake." I didn't usually lie to Paul, because he always seemed to know when I did, but sometimes I could change things a little and get away with it. And I had recited that list to myself so often I almost believed it.

"Mrs. Baca made fried chicken last night," Paul said, forgetting to sound like a sergeant. "And Vinny took me to Baskin-Robbins for ice cream and then to see *The Claw of the Beast*."

"Great." Lucky creep. Why couldn't Elliott have fried that chicken instead of torturing it into a salad?

"What did you and Elliott do after that?"

"Sat around and talked. He told me about growing up in Baltimore, Maryland, during the Depression. He hates the smell of popcorn because sometimes that's all they had to eat when he was a kid."

"Nothing but popcorn? I guess that would get boring." Paul rubbed his eyes, red and swollen from allergies that got worse when we were in the middle of a lot full of weeds. "Where does he work?"

"I don't know."

"You didn't find out how he makes so much money to go around the world and buy all that stuff?"

"I didn't think of it."

Paul whacked the plastic bucket. "Sometimes I think you're really dim, you know what I mean? How can you *not* think about things like that?"

"The subject never came up. What difference does it make?"

"You keep asking that, and I keep telling you it's data. Intelligence that we need." He waved the notebook under my nose.

"I'll find out when I see him again."

"Which is when?"

"Next week, I guess."

"When you go to the opera?" Paul grinned, and it wasn't a nice grin.

"How did you know that?" It was suddenly very stuffy in the blockhouse. I could hardly breathe.

" '*The Magic Flute* is the ideal first opera for a young person,' " Paul mimicked in a singsong voice.

"Just tell me how you found out."

"Elliott talked to your mom, who saw mine in the supermarket. Your mom thinks it's very exciting that you're going to an *opera*, Win. *The Magic Flute* sounds just adorable." Paul flopped his wrist and rolled his eyes. He started to laugh. His eyes were watering, partly because he was laughing so hard, partly because of his allergies. I worked my fists and thought seriously about punching him in the mouth.

"Look, Elliott Deerfield is a good guy. He's got a lot of class, a lot more than Vinny Baca. What do you and Vinny do? Go to horror movies? Big deal. You've never even *been* to an opera, so how do you know what it's like?" My face burned. It did that when I got upset.

Paul began to yowl like a cat with its tail caught in the door. "Yoweeeooo!" he wailed. "I'm an opera singer. Listen!" He yowled some more.

"Just cut it out, okay? Elliott played the record for me, and it's not bad. A lot better in fact than that stupid punk rock craperoo your sister Vanessa worships," I said, getting heated up. "We're going to go over the story together, so we know what's happening. And I have to get dressed up, because everybody dresses up to go to the opera, all the rich people in town and a lot of wealthy tourists, too."

"Golly gosh, Win, maybe you could even rent a tuxedo. Or one of those outfits like English butlers on

TV, with the long tails in the back and the little white bow tie."

"What's the matter with you? I'm not gonna wear no tails. You don't think people really wear stuff like that, do you?"

"Who knows? You never know what turns people on." He cranked up his leering grin again.

I ignored that. "I'm just trying to get this over with. It's not for a long time, anyway. Lots of things could happen in a month. He might change his mind. But if going to some dumb opera is what Elliott wants to do, I guess I have to do it. Anyway you know the rules. If it doesn't work out, in six weeks I just tell Los Amigos and that's it. I'll get somebody new and so will Elliott, no hard feelings." I wondered, though, if Elliott would have hard feelings when he found out I didn't want him for an amigo any more.

Suddenly Paul's voice was serious. "I'd watch it, if I were you."

"Watch what?"

"You hang around with a faggot, people are going to start thinking you're a faggot too."

"*Faggot!*" I roared. "What the hell are you talking about?"

"Oh come on, Winston." Paul called me Winston when he wanted to annoy me. "Don't tell me you're so dim you haven't figured out Elliott Deerfield is gay."

Heat pumped into my face again. "No. I haven't figured that out at all. Just because he's kind of unusual."

"I'll say he's unusual. Likes *opera*? Wears a little *bandanna* around his neck and lots of *jewelry*? Likes to *cook*? Big sport is jumping *rope*? What do you think a confirmed bachelor *is*, anyway? Oh come on, Win, wake up and face facts. Now if that's the way you want to go, that's your decision. But it could be a problem when you start a new school and the word gets around."

"Listen, you never even met this guy. He knows about all kinds of stuff. Indian ruins, for instance. We're going to explore them, camp out and everything." I could hardly believe I was saying this, but it was Paul's fault. Paul was forcing me to defend Elliott, no matter what I really thought. And I wasn't sure what it was that I thought right now.

"Huh," Paul snorted. "I'll bet you anything he wants you to snuggle up in his sleeping bag."

"You're full of crap, Crowser. Right up to your eyeballs. That's why you don't *see* nothing but craperoo."

I shoved open the wooden door to the blockhouse. It had started to rain, and I ran all the way home through the downpour. I didn't care if I got wet, and I knew Paul wouldn't come after me. If there was anything Paul Crowser hated, it was to mess up his camouflage suit.

# FOUR

## HALF A BUBBLE OFF

**M**A RODE up on her bicycle, ducking her head to keep the rain out of her eyes. Her long brown hair was plastered against the daypack slung on her back, and her wet skirt stuck to her legs.

"I thought I'd make it before it started to pour, but I didn't," she panted, wheeling the rusty old bike onto the porch. She grabbed me for a hug. "I don't have to worry about making you wet. You're as soaked as I am."

"Yeah."

She stepped back and looked me over. "You okay, Win?"

"Yeah. Fine."

"You don't sound fine. Want to tell me what's wrong?"

"Argument with Paul. That's all."

"Umm. Sorry to hear that. Anything serious?"

"I don't know if it's serious or not."

Donny was sprawled on the floor in front of the TV, watching a kiddy program. I flipped the dial to a different channel. Donny let out a screech and came up off the floor with his arms windmilling. "I was watching that," he whined. "You get out of here."

"Okay, okay." I turned it back to his channel and went to the kitchen, grabbed a handful of chocolate chip cookies out of a box, mixed some chocolate powder in a glass of milk and cleared a space on the lumpy sofa.

"Did you bring me some?"

"Get them yourself."

"Selfish. I'm telling."

"Go ahead and tell."

He didn't move. I stared at the TV, but I couldn't concentrate on what was happening, even if anything had been worth concentrating on. Thoughts whirred around inside my head like locusts. Suppose what Paul said about Elliott was true? And even if it wasn't, people might think it was, which was just as bad.

The phone rang. "It's for you," Donny said, staring at the TV.

"How do you know?"

"It's Elliott What's-his-face. He called a while ago. I told him you were at the blockhouse."

I picked up the phone. "Elliott Deerfield here," said a deep voice. "Is this Win?"

"Hi, Elliott." The deep voice was a good sign, wasn't it—that Paul was wrong?

We talked about the rain and me getting caught

in it. Then Elliott said he was driving up to Taos on Saturday to watch the kayak races on the Rio Grande, and did I want to go along? More whirring: I did and I didn't.

"Okay," I said finally.

"Good! I'll pick you up at eight o'clock. I'll pack a lunch, or we can grab something along the way."

I went back to the TV and tried not to think of Paul's theory about Elliott, but that was impossible. Ma came out of her bedroom with her hair wrapped in a towel.

"Elliott wants me to go to some kayak races this weekend," I told her.

"He seems like such a nice person," Ma said. "You're lucky to get somebody like that. You'll learn a lot from him, going to the opera and all."

"Why did you tell Mrs. Crowser about that?"

"Wasn't I supposed to? I'm very excited for you. All my life I've wanted to see an opera, and you're the one who's getting to do it."

"Mrs. Crowser told Paul. Friggin' creep gave me a lot of craperoo about it."

"I wish you wouldn't use such crude language. I'm sorry Paul teased you, but some people can't let other people enjoy anything. I think it's absolutely super. There are lots of boys who'd give anything to have a friend like Mr. Deerfield."

"Then maybe I should give somebody else the big break and get another amigo when the six weeks is up. Some real nice, simple person who doesn't think watching TV and making a little grammar mistake once in a while are such big deals." I wished I could tell her what was really bothering me, but I couldn't.

"What's gotten into you? First you can't wait to have an amigo, and then you're snarky about it."

"I wanted somebody ordinary. Somebody with tattoos on his arms who spits on the sidewalk. Somebody like Vinny Baca."

"I'll take him!" Donny chirped, flipping over on his back like a beetle. "Ma, can I have Elliott? When am I going to get an amigo?"

"You can have him if you'll go to the opera in my place."

"Forget it." He flipped back. Smart kid.

"You know what I think?" Ma ran a comb through her hair. "What I think is that you said you'd give it a six-week trial, and this is only the first week. He's probably having just as much trouble adjusting to you as you are to him, did you think about that? Even if you decide you'd rather have somebody else, that's okay, but you aren't being fair. Give it the full six weeks and then make up your mind."

"I don't think I'll last six weeks."

She sighed. "Then call Los Amigos yourself and tell them. Ask them what you should do."

"The kayak races do sound pretty good. Maybe I'll just go to that and then call them."

"It's up to you. But quit complaining." Ma peeled a package of hot dogs, opened a can of beans and put them all into a pan to heat. "Would you go out and clean up the yard after we eat? Mrs. Montoya's dog got in the garbage again." She gave me another hug. "Yuk. Don't you want to change into dry clothes?"

"I don't have no clean ones. I don't have *any* clean ones."

"Guess you'll have to take a couple loads to the laundromat tomorrow, huh?"

I hated to do the laundry. I also hated to clean the yard. Half the garbage on our block seemed to end up in our yard, and strange dogs came to visit. Mostly Mrs. Montoya's black lab, Diablo. Mrs. Montoya was a nice lady who brought us some flowers when we moved in and said she'd keep an eye on Donny and me when Ma was at work. I just wished she'd keep an eye on Diablo.

The mailboxes in our neighborhood all said Romero and Chavez and Martinez and Montoya. The people spoke Spanish to each other, or English with an accent to the rest of us. They had all lived here for a long, long time. This *barrio* was on the West Side. Elliott and most of Ma's housecleaning customers lived on the East Side, where the adobe houses were big and expensive and what Ma called "charming."

Nobody would have called our place "charming." It was small and cruddy—four rooms with water-stained walls and small windows and a gas heater in each room. The flat roof leaked. Crumbling adobe walls fenced in the dusty little yard where a few scraggly weeds survived and muscatel bottles collected. Winos wove up and down our street on their way to a mission for transients, street people who had no jobs, no place to live, no nothing. Guys leaned against broken-down cars that had been up on blocks since we got there. They stopped talking when Ma pedaled by on her bike.

Mrs. Crowser said our neighbors two doors down, the Mondragons, were thieves: a grandma, her three grownup sons and their teenage kids burglarized East-side houses, stealing jewelry and furs and silver and stereos, but nobody ever caught them. Ma said they wouldn't bother us because we had nothing worth stealing. Her philosophy was, "Mind your own business and we'll be all right."

We lived there because we didn't have the money to live anywhere else. Ma dreamed that someday we'd have a place out in the country. Her idea was to find an old house with lots of land around it and fix it up and raise goats and chickens and plant a big garden. She promised Donny we'd have a dog then, too, and maybe a couple of cats. We'd need a pickup, and by then I'd be old enough to drive. I looked forward to that. Ma was a dreamer, but it was her dreams that kept us going.

It was Ma's school night. She wouldn't be home until late, and I had to stay home with Donny with nothing to do after I cleaned up the garbage but watch TV all evening. I decided to forget the argument and call Paul.

"You doing anything with Vinny this weekend?" Probably there was nothing Vinny could come up with better than a kayak race.

"Oh sure. His church is sponsoring a carnival, and Vinny's selling chips and nuts. Mrs. Baca is working at the bingo table, so I'm going to help him. I can't earn money, but I'll probably get lots of stuff free." It was hard to understand him. His mouth was full of something; free chips, probably. "What about you and Elliott?"

"We're going to the kayak races."

"*Kayak* races?" Paul said, making "kayak" sound like something perverted. "*Do* have fun, Win. Just don't let Mr. D. drag you off into the bushes." He started to cackle, and I hung up on him.

Donny had fallen asleep on the floor as he always did. I had to wake him up and get him to pee before I put him in our bed, so we wouldn't end up in the middle of a lake before morning. I crawled in next to him and listened to him talk in his sleep. Nothing he said ever made sense. His language was horrible. He used words Ma would have had a fit over, and I don't mean "friggin' " and "craperoo."

I gave up trying to get to sleep and slid out of bed again. I had a drawer where I kept important things— the pieces of the broken Irish glass, still wrapped in paper napkins, the letter from Michael X. Kelly postmarked four years before telling me he was taking me to the beach and a special notebook. At first I had printed on the cover *The Private Thoughts of Win Kelly*, which was practically an invitation to somebody to read it. Donny, for instance, who was nosy as well as smart. So I pasted a new title on it, *Spelling and Grammar Exercises*, figuring nobody in his right mind would ever look inside a book like that.

I reread the letter from my father. Ma never said much about Michael X. Kelly, except that after they got married he started driving a truck, which was a good job except that he was on the road a lot. "We just drifted apart," she said when I asked her what happened.

I didn't understand how people could just drift apart and have a new family and forget all about the old one. How could he forget about me? I wondered what his new family was like; they would be my half-brothers and half-sisters. When I went out to see him, I'd find out. But I wished he'd write and invite me, so I wouldn't have to wait until I had earned enough money to buy a bike.

And there was Bobby Don Willett, Donny's dad, who was my stepfather for a while before Joe Favello, making me Donny's half-brother too. I always said, "He's my brother." But Donny was no relation to whatever halfs I had out in California.

When Bobby Don married Ma he already had a little girl, Bonnie Marie, who often stayed with us. She was a real pain, especially when Donny was born and she was jealous of all the attention the new baby was getting. Bonnie Marie had been my stepsister, but I didn't know if she still was. Bobby Don got married again and had another family too, his third. This gets very confusing for the kids, but it must be just as confusing for the parents who started it all.

I turned to a clean page in *Spelling and Grammar Exercises*. If Paul could make notes about Elliott, then I could too. But I'd tell the truth about him, like what we really had for dinner, and not what I made up to tell Paul, and the pictures of doors, and Conchita the stuffed maid. I'd write down Elliott's story about eating all that popcorn when he was a kid. There would probably be more stories like that.

I also decided to make some notes on Paul, who if the facts were known, was probably a lot weirder than Elliott. Ma described people she thought were crazy as being "half a bubble off," which I didn't understand until we were in a hardware store and she showed me a carpenter's level. An air bubble in a tube of liquid lines up between two marks if the instrument is level and gets off quick if it isn't.

Paul was *at least* half a bubble off, I thought, but that June he and Elliott were the only people I knew, outside of Ma and Donny. Paul was convinced Elliott was gay; I wondered what Elliott would think about Paul. Probably that he was suffering from shellshock and ought to be given a medical discharge. What was it that made Paul so strange? I decided to observe both of them carefully and see if I could figure them out.

# FIVE

## DIRTY LAUNDRY

**W**E HAD A SYSTEM for laundry:

Ma stuffed all our dirty clothes into plastic trash bags. I lugged two bags to the laundromat and loaded two machines. While they were running I raced home for the next two. By the time I got back the first two loads were ready for the dryer. When they were dry, I hauled them home, went back for the next two. Three round trips between home and X-tra Quality Coin Laundry. It was not fun.

To kill time while the machines churned and whirled, I flipped through old magazines abandoned by other laundromat customers. I was halfway through a story about a child who had triumphed over a horrible birth defect when Vinny Baca bumped through the door with a case of chips to refill the snack machine. He unlocked the machine, dumped the change into a canvas pouch and began stacking little bags of nuts and chips in separate chutes.

I wandered over to watch. Vinny was short and dark with a thick black mustache. He wore a green shirt stretched tight over his broad chest and a baseball cap with "Southwest Snacks" printed on the front in white letters.

"Hi," I said.

"Hello." Vinny glanced up but seemed not to recognize me. We had met only once before.

"I'm Win Kelly, Paul's friend."

"Oh yeah, Win." He stuck out his hand. "How's it going, buddy?"

"Okay."

"What're you doing here?"

"Laundry."

Vinny laughed. "You're kidding! Don't tell me your mother sends you out to do the wash. Real women's libber, huh?"

I didn't want to have to explain that she had no time because she worked three different jobs and went to school besides. Vinny probably wouldn't have been impressed anyway, so I made something up. "I'm just waiting for her here. She's over at the supermarket, and she's afraid somebody might steal our stuff."

Vinny banged the door and locked up the machine with a bunch of keys on a long chain. "You want to play some Pac-Man?"

There were four video games next to the snack machine. Once my grandmother sent me ten dollars for my birthday, and I blew the whole thing playing video games, waiting for the laundry. I felt sick when I got home and all the money was gone. Vinny must have played a lot of these games. He ran up a huge score in no time.

"The trouble is you never win nothing," I complained. "Never win *anything*. No free games or anything."

"No, but you can bet. I could bet you I'll win the next game, or I could bet on somebody else, or I could bet on the score spread, anything. There's a dozen different ways you can gamble, if you want to."

"Yeah."

"Believe me, if there's a way to bet, I'll find it. I'm what you call a compulsive gambler," Vinny said. "It's like an addiction. I used to go to the track every day, but I got it under control now. It's a bad habit, gambling."

"I guess so."

"Bad as drinking. You don't harm your body, but you can sure do a lot of damage to your bank account. My wife made me quit. Ruthie said it was her or the ponies. I picked her, naturally. Ruthie cooks, ponies don't." He laughed at his joke, and I laughed to be polite.

We played another game, but I got tired of competing with somebody who always won, and I didn't even try.

"Gotta go," Vinny said. "You'll make somebody a great wife some day!" He slapped me on the back. "Just fooling," he said and picked up the empty case and climbed into the Southwest Snacks truck.

I couldn't get back into the story of the disfigured child. I was mad because I had to do laundry, which Vinny and probably everybody else believed was a woman's job. I got stuck with it just because Ma had messed up her life.

Laurel Watkins Kelly Willett Favello—and then Watkins again—(just in those names you could see a lot had happened) was born in Stamford, Connecticut, about thirty-four years ago, my age plus twenty. Her father, my grandfather, was a chemical engineer who took the train into New York City every day, while my grandmother went to garden club meetings and things like that. Ma had an older brother who was a lawyer and a sister who was a "proper suburban matron," Ma said, which meant she had two children and stayed home to drive them to cub scouts and ballet lessons. I never met them.

Ma hated all of that, because it was phony and artificial, she said, and she was a rebel. They sent her to boarding school because she wasn't behaving, and she ran away and hitchhiked all the way to California in the 1960s. Her parents were really upset. They expected her to go to college and marry the right kind of man who worked for a big company and be a proper suburban matron like my aunt and my grandmother. She said she had no regrets, but she was sorry she didn't get a college education, because she could have made lots more money and we wouldn't have had such a hard time of it.

Ma told me about living in a commune in Oregon where she learned to do fancy embroidery. That's where she met Michael X. Kelly, who was also a dropout. They smoked a lot of reefer, and she said it really screwed things up for them both, which was why she didn't want me to do it. My father was a war protester and went to Canada to escape the draft. His parents were ashamed of him, because my grandfather John Kelly fought in the South Pacific in World War II and expected Michael X. Kelly to be a good soldier and defend his country too. But my father didn't believe in the war in Vietnam, said it had nothing to do with defending his country, and went to Canada until it was over. Naturally I never told Paul about that.

I used to think a lot about my Watkins grandparents. I had them, but I didn't have them. They sent me birthday cards with money and a check to Ma for all of us every Christmas. I wished we could go visit, but Ma said there wasn't much use thinking about that, because they would never forgive her for throwing her life away.

"Did you throw your life away?"

"By their standards I did."

That bothered me. If I threw my life away, the way Ma's parents said she did hers, would she never forgive me? But I didn't ask it that way. I asked her if she was sure they didn't love her.

"Oh, no," she said. "They love me all right. They just don't like me very much. We're not friends."

I wasn't sure I knew the difference.

Back home I dumped all the clean clothes on the floor in front of the TV. Ma always said I should fold the stuff as soon as it came out of the dryer so it wouldn't wrinkle, but I hated anybody to see me folding clothes, especially women's stuff.

"You do the socks and underwear," I told Donny, "and I'll do the rest."

But it stayed there all evening. If Donny wasn't

going to do his part, forget it. I had to do everything, and Donny did nothing but watch the tube and stuff his face with flufferbanutter sandwiches, bananas glued together with marshmallow fluff and peanut butter on white bread, his main source of nourishment.

# SIX

## ESKIMO ROLL

**D**ONNY YANKED off the covers. "Wake up, wake up, wake up!" he crowed sitting on top of me, as though he were practicing to be the neighborhood rooster. "Elliott's here."

"You're lying."

"No, honest, if you don't believe me, go look. He's standing in the living room *right now*. Elliott says you're supposed to go somewhere."

The kayak races. "What time is it?"

"Eight o'clock."

Ma had said she'd wake me, but she wasn't up yet either. Maybe her alarm didn't go off. She didn't get home until late Friday and Saturday, the nights she played guitar in the restaurant.

I jumped out of bed in my shorts, the holey ones

because everything else was in the laundry. And the laundry was still in the middle of the living room floor.

"Donny," I coaxed, "please go get me some clothes. I need clean shorts and jeans and a shirt. Please."

"Okay." Donny was back in thirty seconds. "Which ones? Everything's there in a big pile. Some of it's still kind of wet."

"I don't care which ones. Whatever you grab."

Donny raced out again. I made the bed and waited. I could hear Donny talking to Elliott. Figuring I'd have to get them myself, I dragged on the jeans I wore the day before, also full of holes. Ma was always too busy fixing other people's clothes to do ours.

Elliott leaned against the doorframe looking like a cowboy. He was dressed in jeans and western boots and a big Stetson and had a bandanna tied around his neck, a red one this time. "Well, good *morning*, Win," Elliott said cheerfully. "Didn't wake you up, did I?"

"Sort of. I'm sorry. It'll only take me a minute to get dressed." I dug through the wads of clothing, found a pair of jeans, still damp, and a wrinkled tee shirt with a picture of a surfer stenciled on the front. In the bathroom I splashed cold water on my face, wet down my hair, and rinsed my mouth. We were out of toothpaste, again. "I'm ready."

"What about breakfast?"

"I don't usually eat breakfast."

"You need something," Elliott said. "It may be a long time until lunch."

I scrounged in the refrigerator and located the pan from last night's supper with some drying-up macaroni and cheese, scraped it all onto a slice of bread, blopped ketchup over it, and slapped another piece of bread on top. "I can eat this on the way."

The reason for taking the Land Cruiser instead of the Chrysler, Elliott explained, was so we could drive up the rough road on the far side of the river and get a better view of the races. It took about an hour. Elliott did most of the talking.

"I've been reading an interesting book," he said. "It describes the major trends of this decade in American culture. I'll lend it to you. It has a lot to do with the world in which you'll spend your future."

The future again. I didn't say anything. I didn't like it when he talked about the future, because I had no idea how to make my future turn out to be what I wanted. Maybe I'd end up being a waiter instead of a writer.

"Are you planning on college?" Elliott was asking.

"If I could figure out where to get the money. A scholarship or something."

"Are you a good student?"

"If I like the teacher okay and the subject, then I do good. If I don't, I don't."

"Apparently you haven't run into any particularly likable English teachers," Elliott muttered.

That was true.

"You'll have to get over that attitude, Win. It's a matter of discipline. Keeping your room neat and your clothes in order, for instance. Finishing what you start. Getting up on time." Blah blah blah; I let it all fly by. Whenever somebody started to lecture, I let my mind drift off away. "I consider discipline fundamental to any sort of achievement," Elliott went on. "I learned about that in the army."

"Army?" That grabbed my attention. "Were you in the army?"

"Yes."

"Did you get wounded or anything? Were you a hero?" That was the kind of question Paul would ask. I pictured Elliott charging up on a beach, blasting away with a machine gun, hitting the dirt when the enemy blasted back, digging a foxhole and diving in, crawling out to rescue a buddy under fire.

"I hate to disappoint you, Win, but I never left the States." The picture vanished. "I was lucky to get in at all. I have bad eyesight, and at first they wouldn't take me. This was World War II, of course. All my friends were joining up, being sent overseas, and I was still in Baltimore, working in the shipyards. So when they called me up again for a physical, I made up my mind I'd pass. I took a good look at the eye chart and memorized the first few lines under the big E. Then I hid my glasses. The doctor said, 'Tell me what you see on the chart,' and I recited the letters, and he passed me. After basic training I was assigned to the automotive pool and ended up chauffeuring the big brass around Washington, D.C., in a jeep."

What a story. Not the kind Paul would go for. "How come you don't wear glasses no more except to read?"

"*Any more.*"

"Any more."

"I wear contact lenses for distance. The others are for close work."

Wasn't it just women who wore contact lenses? I
changed the subject. "I've thought about joining the
Navy," I said. "To travel. That's my big goal in life,
travel."

I hadn't really thought about it much, but when
I told Elliott, it seemed as though it had been on my
mind for a long time. I'd travel, and then I'd write
stories about the places I saw.

"Well, joining the Navy is one way to do it."

"You've traveled a whole lot, huh?"

"Yes. I've been to six of the seven continents.
There's a scientific vessel that sails down to Antarctica
once a year, and I'll probably go along some time and
make it seven. Meantime, I'm planning to do a safari
in Kenya and Tanzania this fall."

"I guess it takes a lot of money to go all those
places."

"It does, but then you must remember I have
nobody but myself to look after. I told you, I'm very
selfish. I save up and I go where I want, when I want.
That's one of the advantages of being a bachelor."

Maybe I'd be a bachelor: Stay single and see the
world.


Elliott knew the best place to watch the kayaks—
from a mesa above the rapids. He popped open two
camp stools and handed me a pair of binoculars and
showed me how to focus. Every few seconds a kayak
would squirt through the narrow gorge and hit the
foaming rapids. It didn't take much to flip one upside
down, but the kayaker would roll it right over, coming
up and furiously dipping his two-ended paddle on one
side and then the other.

"That's called an eskimo roll," Elliott explained. "One of the first things you have to learn in a kayak is how to turn over and come up again."

"I'd be scared."

"It's frightening," Elliott agreed, "but the way to control fear is to face it."

"Are you scared of much?"

"Maybe not of *much*, but certainly of some things. Mostly, though, it's people that scare me."

"Muggers and murderers and things like that?"

"No, weak people. They're more dangerous than the malicious ones, I've found. You can see the bad ones coming and figure out what to do about them, but weak people are harder to detect. They sneak up and take advantage of you. You get pulled in, like quicksand. Have you ever been caught in quicksand?"

I said I hadn't.

"I have. Once I was hiking in a streambed, sloshing along through a narrow canyon that had some absolutely stunning wildflowers. I was taking pictures and not paying enough attention to where I was walking, and I stepped in what looked like ordinary sand. But it was as though I had put my leg into fast-setting cement."

"That's quicksand?"

"Yes. Just an innocent-looking mixture of sand and water, and it sucks you right in. Let me tell you, I was stuck, all the way up to my thigh. That was scary! I really thought it was the end! But then a couple of hikers came along and got some logs out to me, and I finally managed, little by little, to work free. I was there for hours. Lost the camera, too." He shook his head, remembering. "And some people are like that. They seem innocent and friendly, and when you're not watching—whoosh!—you're stuck. And they make you feel guilty when you try to pull away."

I wondered if I knew anybody like that. Another volley of kayaks shot through the canyon. Elliott asked if I was getting hungry. I wasn't *getting* hungry; I was *always* hungry.

"Time for sustenance, then."

He opened the back of the Land Cruiser and pulled out a small folding table. Built onto the rear door was a little wooden cabinet with slots for dishes, silverware, cups, and glasses. The front of the cabinet dropped down to form a shelf. While I set up the table and spread a checkered cloth on it, Elliott unpacked the lunch. Out of the cooler came two cans of Dr Pepper, "a rare vintage, especially for you," and a small bottle of wine. Then he unwrapped a loaf of French bread, a container of butter, a chunk of cheese, four plums, and a thick slab of something gray and strange.

"What's this?"

"Paté. Try it on a piece of bread."

"What's it made out of?" I wished there was ketchup, but Elliott didn't believe in ketchup.

"Never mind. Just try it."

It would have been better with ketchup. When I finished Elliott told me it was made of ground-up liver. I was sorry that I asked and that he told me.

The best part of the meal was the mocha cake, baked by Elliott himself, and not even from a mix.

We watched more kayaks dance over the foaming rapids, and then we packed up everything and started back the long way because Elliott said he wanted to see the wildflowers. One more thing not to tell Paul.

Elliott kept a book called *Roadside Wildflowers of Southwest Uplands* in the glove compartment, and whenever we spotted something he'd tell me how to look it up.

"Yeah, but I don't know nothing about them."

"Win, what you just said was that you *do* know something. Were you aware of that?"

"Double negative?"

"Right."

"I don't know anything, then."

"That can be remedied." He pulled off the road. "One way to learn is by taking photographs."

He unpacked a complicated camera from a leather bag, fitted on a special lens, and showed me how to set the f-stop and decide on the shutter speed. He talked about depth of field and backlighting. After all the instruction I finally got to snap a picture of some little red flowers called Scarlet Bugler being buzzed by a squadron of hummingbirds.

I liked the names of the plants: Dodder, Indian Paintbrush, Devil's Hair, Mugwort, and Goat's Beard, a puffball like a giant dandelion. The book said that "Skyrocket Gilia is often confused with Scarlet Bugler," but Elliott was never confused. Elliott knew them all, and every time we spotted a different kind, he stopped and I flipped through the book to find out what it was. Then Elliott let me out to take a picture.

"Did you know," I asked him, "that you can eat the fruit of the prickly pear cactus and even make jelly out of it?"

"I've done that," Elliott said. "I may even have a jar or two at home for you to try."

Should have guessed.

We came to a field of purple flowers, thousands of them, so that the whole meadow was purple. I found it fast: Rocky Mountain Iris. I took a close-up, and then we changed lenses and set up a long-distance shot of the meadow.

"Beautiful, isn't it?"

"It's sure pretty. Would it be okay to pick some?"

We wrapped the stems in wet paper towels to keep fresh until we got home.

Ma had her sewing machine set up in the living room, and when we walked in she was roaring through a stack of mutilated jeans for DenimWerx. She jumped up and rushed around straightening the messy room. Everything in the house looked as though it had been found in a junk pile, which it probably had. Ma had a habit of dragging home things that she thought she'd fix up some day, like old chairs with the seats missing, but somehow she never got around to it. We had hauled it all down in a truck from Colorado.

"Hello, Mr. Deerfield," she said, balling up the jeans heaped on the sprung-out sofa so he'd have a place to sit.

"Please call me Elliott, will you? I just wanted to drop Win off and say hello."

She smiled nervously and kept on fussing. "Did you have a good time?" I whipped the bunch of irises out from behind my back and watched the smile spread all over her face. "Oh, Win," she said, "they're real pretty. Thank you." She started toward the kitchen to find something to put them in. "Would you like some herb tea—Elliott?"

I was surprised when he said yes. The ceiling was low, and he had to stoop to come through the door. He hunched in the space Ma cleared on the sofa and waited while she made the tea.

Donny was sprawled on the floor, his usual position, watching TV, his usual activity. It's what he did all the time, it's what I did most of the time too, and suddenly it embarrassed me. Elliott had to talk louder because of the television. If I turned it off, Donny would howl and carry on. Ma didn't seem to notice it. She had a way of tuning things out. I managed to ease down the volume a little at a time, stopping when I saw Donny cranking up to complain.

The phone rang. "It's Paul," Donny announced without taking his eyes off the tube.

I answered it. "Kelly? Report to the blockhouse in eight minutes," Paul said in his army sergeant's voice.

"I can't right now." I was in no mood for that game.

"Why not?"

"Elliott's here. We just got back from the kayak races."

"What are you doing?"

"Uh. Having tea." I could have kicked myself for not thinking faster.

Paul laughed his ugly laugh. "*Tea?* Well, be sure to notice how he holds the cup, Win. If he's got his pinky up in the air, then you know for *sure*." He laughed again, crazily. "Call me as soon as he leaves."

I was afraid to look at Elliott when Ma handed him the mug.

# SEVEN

■ · ■

# WAR STORIES

**R**EPORT on the kayak races," Paul said.
"Start at the beginning, when he picked you up."

Paul had switched to his summer uniform, a tee shirt printed in brown and pink desert camouflage and a pair of dark green sneakers he claimed were government issue to soldiers in Central America.

"Well," I began carefully, "he got there before I was up, and he had to wait while I got dressed, but then—"

"Clothes," Paul said. "What about Elliott's clothes?

"Jeans." I didn't mention the designer label on the hip pocket. "Boots and a Stetson."

"Was he wearing that cute little bandanna around his neck, too?"

"No," I lied.

"I think you're lying," he said.

"I didn't really notice," I lied again.

"Just admit he was wearing a bandanna and get it over with."

"I guess he was. But his hat was so tall, *he's* so tall, he actually had to *stoop* to come through the door. Elliott is much too big for our house!"

"My, my!" he said sarcastically. "Okay, then what?"

"We went in the Land Cruiser because we were taking rough back roads, no ordinary car could go there, and we watched the races from the top of the mesa. These guys strapped inside kayaks with helmets and life vests and rubber suits, flipping all over the place. It was pretty exciting. You'd never get me in one of those things."

"It doesn't sound exciting," Paul said. "It sounds boring. What did you talk about? Did you find out how he got to be rich?"

"No," I said casually, "but he told me about his wartime experiences."

"Old Elliott was in World War II?"

"Yes."

"Well, where was he? Overseas? Doing what?"

I remembered my picture of Elliott charging up on a beach under enemy fire, and I wanted Paul to see that same picture, or a better one, even if it wasn't real. "I don't think he wanted to talk about it," I said. "He drove an armored vehicle—"

"He drove a *tank*?"

"Something like that, yes." I amazed myself. I couldn't get around a bandanna, but I could invent a tank. This wasn't really a lie, though, because it had to be a special kind of vehicle if the army brass was riding in it, and possibly it was armored. "I guess he had a pretty rough time. You know what it was like." We had both seen movies with tanks rolling through war-torn villages and being blown up when a grenade was lobbed through the hatch.

Paul studied me suspiciously. "You sure he drove a tank?"

"Look, hey, I wasn't there or anything. I mean, I can't prove it. Why don't you ask him yourself?"

"I will, when I meet him," Paul said. "Not that I'm accusing you of lying about anything this important. I just want to hear it from the horse's mouth."

"Naturally," I said.

"What rank was he?"

"Captain."

Paul's eyes bugged. "Be serious! A *captain*?"

"Captain," I insisted.

I was getting in too deep. On the one hand it would be good if Paul could meet Elliott and see for himself how big and masculine he was, and that he did not look at all gay, but on the other hand, what if Paul started asking him all kinds of direct questions and found out I had made up a lot of stuff, like being a captain. Even worse, what if Paul had been right about Elliott all along? I could hardly stand to think of it.

"So go on about the kayak races."

"We watched them for a while, and then we ate lunch—"

"Another faggoty gourmet special? Tea and crumpets?"

"I bet you don't even know what a crumpet *is*."

"It's what English fags eat."

"Meatloaf and chocolate cake and Dr Pepper."

"And then what?"

"We took the back road home, and Elliott showed me how to use his Japanese camera, how to figure out the f-stops and the speed and all. Elliott is almost a professional photographer, you know."

"What kind of camera?"

"Konica. He has special lenses for it, zoom, wide-angle, the works. I got to use the close-up lens."

"What were you taking close-ups of?"

"Wildflowers," I said, straight out, just like that. I will never know why I lied about some things and told the truth about others. It didn't make sense, but that's what I did.

"*Wildflowers?*" That set Paul off. I knew it would. It was okay to say we were taking pictures, but I should have said we were using the zoom lens and saw an elk or something. An elk is okay, a Scarlet Bugler is not. Paul laughed so hard he almost fell off the cement block. I wished he had, and done himself some kind of injury that would have kept him from laughing for months.

"It was like a lesson in botany. He says the best way to learn about something is to take a picture of it." I was so embarrassed I wanted to cry, but I wasn't going to let Paul see that. I should have kept on with the war stories. My mouth was still running. "Next weekend we're going to the track," I said.

"The *race* track?"

"Of course." Back on top again. I knew Paul loved horses. If there was still a cavalry, he'd want to join. "Elliott knows all about horses. He, uh, he used to raise them. You ever been to the track, Paul?"

Paul shook his head. "Vinny used to say he was going to take me, but we never got around to it. He said he made a promise and couldn't go."

"You know what the promise was?" I asked innocently.

"No."

I decided not to tell him. I didn't need to. "Elliott's going to show me how to use his camera to take pictures of the horses, which ought to be pretty interesting."

Finally I had hit the right spot and had the satisfaction of watching Paul eat his heart out. Besides, the races might be fun. All I had to do now was talk Elliott into it.

# EIGHT

## WINNING

**E**LLIOTT sounded pleased that I called him. Up to now it had been the other way around: he called me.

"I just wondered what you were doing," I said. I knew it wouldn't be anything normal.

"Reading about unicorns," Elliott replied. "I just bought a handsome new book on the subject. Absolutely fascinating. There are all sorts of myths and lore that exist about unicorns. Have you ever seen a picture of that famous tapestry, 'The Unicorn in Captivity'? It's extraordinarily beautiful."

That was a coincidence, because I liked unicorns too. For my birthday in January Ma had bought me a card with a painting of a unicorn, and I kept the card in my private drawer. I wished she'd make me a jacket like Bobby Don's, except I knew I could never wear it to school. It was not a good idea to wear anything unusual to school—not in Colorado, probably not here either.

I could imagine what would happen if I reported this conversation to Paul: "Well, what did you and Elliott talk about today, Win?" "Unicorns, Paul. We both like unicorns a lot." "*Unicorns?*" Howls of laughter.

"I've been up since five o'clock, working on a report for one of my clients," Elliott was saying. "Thank goodness it's out of the way."

"What kind of report?"

"I'm a consultant for a manufacturer of scientific equipment used to locate underwater oil deposits."

"Are you a scientist?"

"Geologist, actually."

A geologist! You couldn't be what Paul said Elliott was and be a geologist, could you? If I got him to talk about rocks and stuff, that might make up for the wildflowers and the opera and the gourmet cooking.

"Do you like caves?" Elliott was asking. "We could make a trip down to Carlsbad Caverns some time. Absolutely spectacular. Especially the bat flights at sunrise and sunset."

"Sounds good." I wasn't sure about the bats, but the rest of it was so interesting I almost didn't care about the track any more. Except that I had told Paul we were going.

"Elliott," I began, "you said I should call you if I got any ideas of something I'd like to do. So I'm calling."

"Well, I'm delighted! What do you have in mind?"

"I was wondering if we could go to the track sometime."

"The race track? I've never been attracted to that kind of thing, but if it's something you want to do, I'm sure we can arrange it."

We arranged it. Elliott picked me up the next Saturday afternoon and we drove out to The Downs.

"How did you get to be a geologist?" I asked him.

"Accidentally. It wasn't what I wanted to be at all. I dreamed of being a writer, if you can imagine anything more different. But growing up during the Depression, I had to have a more practical goal. So I majored in the only field in which I could qualify for college money, and that happened to be geology. You also have to be almost a little crazy to be a writer. But someday, when I'm retired, I'm going to write. You'll see."

We parked the car and followed the crowd toward the entrance, but I was not seeing any of it. *He wants to be a writer too* thundered in my head; *you have to be a little crazy*.

"How come you have to be crazy?"

"For what?" He had already forgotten our conversation.

"To be a writer. You said you weren't crazy enough to be a writer. Why do you have to be crazy?"

"Because then you're in charge of the world. The imaginary world in your head. First you create chaos, and then you bring order out of the chaos. You can do anything you want to, as long as it makes sense. It's like being God, and you have to be other than what most people consider normal to play God even for a few hours a day at a typewriter. Much easier to stick with schists and gneisses in the real world. Rocks. Besides," he said, "very few writers make much money, and as you know by now, I'm fond of certain luxuries."

Elliott bought a racing form and a program, and we took our time looking around. Near the finish line was a large electronic board with a list of all the horses that would run in the next race, by number, and more numbers across the top of the board that were constantly changing. Those were the odds, Elliott explained, so you could tell which horses were being favored to win, right up to the time the race started. Behind us were rows and rows of windows with long lines of people waiting to place their bets, like customers at a bank. As bets were placed, the numbers changed on the board.

"Are you going to bet?"

"I'm not a gambler, at least at this sort of thing. When I risk my money it's because I think I have a good chance of getting a decent return on it. At the track, frankly, I feel as though I'd be throwing it away."

"But the point of coming to the track is to bet, isn't it?"

"I guess it is for most of these people. But not for me. Let's go look at the horses."

We found the paddock where the jockeys and trainers were getting ready for the next race. "Which horse do you think will win?" I asked him. They all looked beautiful to me.

"I have no idea." He unpacked his camera and fitted on a lens. This time he didn't lecture on how to operate the camera but instead got involved in composition. The Rule of Thirds, in which you mentally divide the scene into thirds both across and up and down, and arrange the picture according to those imaginary horizontal and vertical lines.

A man in a bright red jacket and a little black cap came out and blew a horn. A bell rang, and we all rushed to the finish line. "They're off!" yelled the announcer. Seconds later a blur of yellow, blue, red, purple, green streaked by. No chance to focus the camera, let alone think of the Rule of Thirds. I couldn't tell which was the winner until the results flashed on the board. Those who had picked right went to the windows to collect their money, and everybody lined up to place their next bet.

Every twenty minutes there was another race. Elliott and I took pictures, passing the camera back and forth. With the telephoto lens I caught the tense face of the jockey at the starting gate and the happy grin of a winner. Otherwise it got pretty boring. You had to care which horse won to make it interesting, and if you didn't bet, you didn't care. I wasn't going to have much to tell Paul.

"Let's take a look at what the experts say." Elliott put on his half glasses and studied the racing form. "Listen to this, Win. Number Four, Lucky Devil, is picked as the favorite here, and the board shows he's favored two to one. We could put two dollars on Lucky Devil to win and have a reasonable chance of getting our money back. Then we could pick one of the longer shots to place, and another to show, and see what happens."

"You mean we're going to bet?"

"I suppose it wouldn't hurt to invest a few dollars in this as an educational experience. Let's say ten dollars maximum for the afternoon. Okay?"

"O-kay!"

We got in line at one of the betting windows. I scanned the crowd through the telephoto, watching people who didn't know I was watching them. Then about five lines over I saw Vinny Baca. I wondered if he had not told me the truth about quitting, or if he had started gambling again. He didn't see me. I pressed the button. The shutter clicked.

"What were you taking a picture of?"

"Just the people standing in line."

"Did you remember to slow down the shutter or open up the f-stop? The light's very low in here."

"I forgot."

"Then I think you wasted a shot."

"Probably." But maybe not.

Elliott placed the bets with the woman at the window—his bets, but he insisted they were for both of us—and we went back outside to watch the race, the little you could actually see of it. I held the tickets and tried to remember which numbers and colors we were looking for. The announcer reported it all in a fast, high voice, and the blur of color at the end was pretty exciting. Lucky Devil finished third, so we didn't win anything on that one. Deep Fever trailed behind, but Finn's Glory came in second.

"So there you have it," Elliott said. "We collect three dollars and sixty cents on Finn's Glory. We bet six dollars and won three-sixty, so our net loss on that was two-forty. We have seven-sixty left. What shall we do?"

"Bet again."

He let me do the picking. Sometimes I picked because I liked the name of the horse or the jockey, and sometimes I did it "scientifically," reading the racing form and following the odds. We won some and lost some. I found out one thing: it was fun to win, but it felt bad to lose. And then, on the next to last race, we won eighteen dollars!

"Now what?" Elliott asked.

Maybe we were getting lucky. Maybe we could hit it again. "What do *you* want to do? It's your money."

"You were responsible for that big win. You decide."

Vinny Baca waited in line again at one of the betting windows. I wondered how his luck was going and remembered how bad he said it could get, when he couldn't quit. Suddenly I was tired of the whole thing. "Let's go," I said to Elliott. "Let's not bet that money we won. Let's do something else."

"Fine with me. We have enough to get something to eat and see a movie," he said.

We went to The Whole Enchilada, a restaurant with hanging green plants and paintings for sale by local artists, and ordered gigantic burgers, mine with cheese and bacon, his with green chili. I was surprised to see Elliott eating anything so ordinary. We had chocolate shakes, too.

While we ate he told me about a cabin he built in the Sierras all by himself, how he used to go there on weekends, and how once he got snowed in and ran out of food except for canned sardines and didn't think he'd get out alive. Now he couldn't stand sardines any more than popcorn.

Elliott had a lot of good stories. Someday he'd write them down, but meanwhile I planned to put them in my notebook. I wasn't ready yet to tell him about being a writer too.

# NINE

## CARICATURE

**T**HE PLAZA buzzed with people. That's the center of Santa Fe, where kids showed off on skate boards and roller skates, tourists strolled with ice cream cones, and locals sat on the benches and watched it all. Under the portal of the Governor's Palace dozens of Indians spread their turquoise and silver jewelry and pots on blankets. People with cameras hunkered down to examine the pots and try on the jewelry, and the Indians waited silently for them to make up their minds. Across the street a small crowd gathered around a caricaturist beneath a striped umbrella. He was drawing a caricature of a woman sitting in a canvas chair. The woman was asking questions, which he answered while he sketched, and a television crew recorded the scene.

Paul and I worked our way up front for a better view. The cameraman panned across the crowd. Paul mugged when it looked as though the TV camera was pointed in his direction. The caricaturist handed the woman her portrait. She pretended to be surprised and held it up. "Who'd like to have a caricature done on television?"

Paul yelled, "He would!" and gave me a shove.

I could have killed him. I tried to argue, but the woman was already pointing a microphone at me. "Wonderful!" she said. "What's your name?"

"Win Kelly."

"Win, welcome to ArtScene, Santa Fe's own show about Santa Fe's own artists, featuring today Al Johnson, caricaturist here on the Plaza for twelve years. Have you ever been on TV before?"

"No, ma'am." She steered me toward the canvas chair.

"Don't look at me, look over there," growled the cartoonist in the big straw hat. "And hold still."

I held still. Out of the corner of my eye I could see Paul making goofy faces.

"You've got great freckles, kid," the artist said.

Was I supposed to say thank you? I didn't know, so I didn't say anything.

The woman interviewer kept up her questions to the caricaturist, asking what he did in the winter, whether people took his art work seriously, and what celebrities he had drawn. Finally he tore the page off his sketch pad. "Here, Bill, what do you think?"

"My name's Win. Win Kelly." I glanced at the sketch: spiky red hair, green eyes, freckles splattered like mud, a big grin with too many teeth. It looked like Alfred E. Newman from *Mad Magazine*.

"Tell us what you think of this," the woman insisted, taking the sketch out of my hands and holding it up for the camera.

"Great," I said.

"Yours to keep," the artist said.

Crowser was laughing like crazy. "We can hang it in the blockhouse," he said. "Unless you want to frame it and give it to old Elliott."

The TV crew packed up their gear. The caricaturist attracted a new victim. An old Indian woman with a wrinkled face shuffled through the crowd silently offering turquoise necklaces dangling from both arms. A beautiful woman in expensive clothes strolled by arm in arm with a familiar-looking man. "Jessica Lange and Sam Shepard," Paul said, nudging me. "I saw Robert Redford here a couple of weeks ago."

Seeing movie stars reminded us that if we had had any money we would have gone to a show, but we didn't. Instead we wandered in and out of stores. Paul loved going into shops where he knew kids were not welcome, like the ones that sold silver and crystal and expensive leather. The sales people looked nervous, and then Paul would explain that we were cousins shopping for a birthday present for our grandmother. He called her Granny Applesauce, and when the saleswoman asked him about the name, and they almost always did, he launched into a fantastic story about how he called her that when he was a little kid and the name had stuck. He said she had nineteen cats and drove a government surplus mail truck. He had the lady

at the sports store convinced we were going to buy
Granny Applesauce a fishing rod for her trip to Alaska.
They never knew whether to believe him or not. Even
I half-believed him—and I knew he was making it up.

We got tired of that and started home.

"You and Elliott go to the races?"

"Yeah. What did you and Vinny do over the
weekend?" I thought of Vinny in line at the betting
window.

"Went out to the firing range for target practice."

"Was it fun?"

"Sure. Vinny's *real* good. He was a rifleman in
Vietnam, got medals for it and everything. He belongs
to the National Rifle Association. He wants to teach
my mom how to handle a gun in order to defend herself. Vinny says everybody ought to know how to use a
gun."

"Ma says she wouldn't have a gun in the house.
She says it's dangerous to have a loaded gun around,
and if it isn't loaded, what good is it?"

"Vinny says guns aren't dangerous, *people* are
dangerous." That sounded like something Elliott
would say. "She's probably worried about Donny
getting hold of it. But if Donny got lessons in how to
use a gun, he'd respect it. Vinny'd teach him, I bet,
even if you don't want to learn."

Better to drop it, I decided. The last thing we
needed was Donny running around with a loaded gun.

We were almost at the blockhouse. "Let's stop in
here and smoke," Paul said.

The blockhouse was like an oven, so hot we could
hardly stand it in there. Paul had started smoking. He

couldn't do it at home, except at night in his backyard tent after everybody was asleep.

"I'm going to Dallas to see my father," Paul said, acting as though he wasn't excited at all, as though this was something that happened all the time.

"When are you going?" I matched his calmness, thinking how I'd feel if I were going to San Diego. I wouldn't have been able to keep quiet about it all afternoon the way Paul had.

"Couple weeks. Mom is dead against it, but Dad sent me a plane ticket, and I'm going."

"How come your mom doesn't want you to go?"

Paul shrugged. "You know how it is. People get divorced and then each one tries to make you feel you have to choose that one, and they get mad if you seem to be choosing the other one. She keeps crying and saying, 'You don't understand. You just don't understand.'"

"Understand what?"

"That's exactly what I keep asking her, and she says it's too hard to explain, I'll understand when I'm older. She says he promised he'd stay away, but now he's broken his promise, and she's not going to let him near me. And I say I want to see him, he's my father, it's my right to see him, and she yells back that if I knew what he was like I wouldn't be so anxious to see him and then she starts to bawl again and says for her sake I shouldn't go."

"Can she really keep you from going?"

"I don't know. Maybe my dad can force her to let me."

"So what are you going to do?"

Paul sighed. "I don't know."

"Have you asked your sister? Maybe she knows what's going on."

"I did. Vanessa doesn't know either. She thinks Mom's making a lot of it up because she's jealous and she's scared I'll decide I want to go live with him or something. Anyway Vanessa's furious because he invited me and not her."

"So what are you going to do?"

"You already asked me that. I told you I don't know." He lit another cigarette and practiced blowing smoke rings, and I sweated. "How's old Elliott?"

"Fine." I told him about the races, but not about seeing Vinny Baca.

"Elliott treat you to another gay gourmet delight after the race?"

I pretended not to hear. That was Ma's suggestion: "Just don't *hear* him when he says something ugly." I still hadn't told her what kinds of things Paul said—that Elliot was gay—or that I was worried Paul might be right.

"Are you listening, Kelly? I asked if he fed you more faggot food."

This time I heard him.

"You think everybody who's different is a faggot. And I'm telling you cooking doesn't have anything to do with being gay or straight or anything else. Liking to cook is about liking food. It's not about sex."

"Said the banana to the doughnut."

"You afraid of catching queerness, Paul? Something that floats around like salmonella in the tuna-fish?"

"I don't know how you catch it. But if I was you, I'd be plenty worried."

"I'm not worried," I said, which wasn't true. I changed the subject. "Elliott's going to be a writer someday. When he was a kid he wanted to be a writer but you couldn't make any money at that, so he got to be a geologist instead. So when he retires in a few years he's going to write."

"What's he going to write? *Fairy* tales?" And there was that ugly laugh again. I was instantly sorry I had told him anything at all.

# TEN

## YARD SALE

"**I**'M TURNING over a new leaf," Ma announced. "No more collecting junk we don't need. No more dragging home trash that never gets transformed to treasure. As a matter of fact, Winston Allen Kelly, you and I are going to clean out this place and have one enormous yard sale. We should have done it before we left Durango, instead of carting it all down here. This was supposed to be a fresh start, and it's not a fresh start when you bring your past with you."

"Sounds good to me." It would be nice to get rid of the junk, except I wasn't sure we'd have anything left.

"We'll do it next Saturday," she said. "I'll put an ad in *Thrifty Nickel*, and I'll make some signs for you and Donny to put up around the neighborhood. Whatever we don't sell, we'll give to Goodwill."

"Give *back* to Goodwill," I said. "That's probably where it came from in the first place."

Ma got Donny to collect all his old toys and games while I pulled stuff out of closets and she tackled the boxes stacked in her bedroom. You could hardly get past the cartons to reach her bed and dresser.

"My whole life is in those boxes," she said. "And most of yours, too."

There were things she was going to work on someday, clothes Donny had outgrown that I had outgrown first, pages torn from magazines, old sketch pads and brushes and dried-up tubes of paint, ragged sheet music and song books, bunches of snapshots—all jumbled together in boxes labeled "good stuff" and "old stuff." I don't know how she decided which was which.

It took a long time, most of one night. Some of the things she found made her sad, and some made her happy. She flipped through a sketch pad full of geometric designs, swirling leaves and flowers, and pen-and-ink drawings of people: a girl picking a flower, a baby sucking its thumb, an old woman leaning on a cane, a man pushing a supermarket cart. I had never seen these sketches before.

"I used to think I was going to be an artist. But it's hard to make a living."

"You're good, Ma! I didn't know you could do stuff like this."

"Maybe someday I'll go back to it. Might as well put them on that pile over there for the garbage."

"You mean you're going to throw them out? Why don't we sell them?"

"I can't imagine who'd want them."

"Somebody might. I'll just put them out and see, and if nobody buys them I want to keep them."

"Up to you."

We went through the house putting tags on all the derelict chairs and tables that Ma was going to fix up someday but didn't. She would see all over again the "possibilities," as she called them, and I'd have to remind her that she promised to be hard-hearted and get rid of everything we were not actually using.

Over the Fourth of July, when Ma had off, we worked on it, piling things in the living room that would go into the yard sale. Ma called Paul's mother and invited her to put their things in with ours to make it a really huge sale.

Friday afternoon Vanessa drove over in their old Subaru with a ton of stuff, which I had to help unload. Vanessa specialized in weirdness. She had on a black sweat shirt turned inside out with the neck and arms torn off, neon pink socks, long dangling earrings. Her hair was scrambled and her makeup made her look bruised and wounded, as though she had been attacked by a wild beast. She always had a crush on whatever rock star was new and hot and collected all the albums and posters until the next one came along. Ma said having brothers and sisters gave you experience in dealing with the real world, but I could not believe Vanessa Crowser was the real world.

I had told Elliott what we were doing, explaining that I wouldn't be able to come over on Saturday because I'd be busy all day. He said maybe Sunday we could go to the outdoor sculpture show if I wanted to. Early Saturday morning, while we were hauling "merchandise" out of the house, he showed up with two cartons of magazines and asked if we'd like to have them, mostly copies of *Smithsonian* and *Scientific American*. He said he couldn't bear to throw them away, and we could keep whatever money we got from them.

Then he saw the sketchbook with Ma's drawings.

"Where in the world did you get these?"

"They're Ma's. She said to throw them out, but I thought maybe somebody might buy them."

"I'll say somebody might buy them!" Elliott said. "Where is your mother?"

Ma came out with an armload of clothes to spread out on the adobe wall, and Elliott went right over, waving the sketchbook. He told her that she had a great deal of talent and should be an artist, and he wanted to buy the whole sketchbook and how much would she take for it. She said she didn't have any idea, anything at all would be fine. He wrote Ma a check for forty dollars, which was five dollars apiece, and said he felt he was robbing her. He promised that if he ever sold or traded any of them for something else, he would give her the difference.

Elliott came and went while Paul and Vanessa were picking up another load of their stuff. In a way I wished they had been there to see him getting delirious over Ma's drawings, but on the other hand I didn't have the energy to deal with introducing them and worrying what Paul would say afterwards.

Ma did a good job of arranging displays, turning our yard into a funky outdoor department store. Mrs. Crowser put yellow tags on their stuff and green on ours, to make it easy to sort out the money. She had to go to work at the beauty shop, but she left Vanessa and

Paul to help out. Donny and I had stuck Ma's signs all over the neighborhood. The sale wasn't supposed to start until nine o'clock, and we were busy until the last minute setting things up, but by eight o'clock people were coming to look around.

It was a strange feeling to have people poking around our things and whispering that they'd never have a thing like *that* in their house. Clothes and dishes sold fast, and then a bald man with a panel truck made a deal for all our broken-down furniture—not as much as Ma hoped to get if she sold it piece by piece, until just before noon when some kids arrived to see if we had any games. Paul knew them, because they went to his school. He introduced us: Steve, Tony, Jamie, Ross.

While these guys were standing around talking and looking macho, a girl came into the yard, dark-haired with blue eyes, about my age. She looked familiar; maybe I had seen her at the laundromat or the supermarket. But it wasn't her hair or her eyes that I observed first. She had big breasts, *huge* breasts, which I could not help noticing even though she wore a baggy man's shirt with shoulders that dropped way down her arms. I heard Paul's ugly laugh. They were all staring at the girl and watching me.

"Do you have any books or magazines?" she asked, and I pointed to the boxes of Elliott's scientific journals. Then I heard Vanessa somewhere behind me say, in a low voice, "Mooooo." Her voice wasn't low enough, though; the girl must have heard her. She froze for a second and then knelt down and concentrated on the magazines. She stayed there a long time.

Vanessa got busy with a woman who wanted to haggle over the price of a couple of Mrs. Crowser's rusty pans. I went over to see if the girl wanted to buy any of Elliott's magazines, or if she was just going to keep her face buried in them.

"Hi," I said in a croaky voice, knowing the guys were watching and snickering.

She looked up. Pretty eyes. "Hi. Are these yours?"

"They belonged to a friend of mine. Do you want to buy any?"

"Maybe. These are terrific. I'm looking for articles about butterflies and whales and seals."

"Have you found any yet?"

"A couple. Would you mind helping me look? If you don't have something else to do."

So what could I say? Tell her no, I don't have time? I hunkered down next to her and started going through the magazines.

"You just check the index," she said. "Who is this friend of yours?"

"Which friend? You mean Paul?"

"I know him and his cretinish cohorts, all right," she said grimly. "I mean Elliott M. Deerfield."

"How do you know his name?" I didn't even know he had a middle initial.

"It's right here on the address label."

"Oh." I felt foolish. I hadn't noticed the labels. "So who is he? A scientist?"

"A geologist. He's a consultant for underwater oil drilling companies."

"I'll bet he knows about whales and seals then too."

"Probably. He seems to know about practically everything."

"How did you get to be friends?"

"We're members of Los Amigos."

"Oh, I know some kids who belong to that, and they have really dull amigos. You're lucky. I'll bet you do interesting things with him. Do you go rock hounding?"

"No." I wondered what she'd say if I told her we were going to the opera. She'd probably think that was okay. "What's your name?"

"Heather Key."

"I'm Win Kelly."

"I've seen you at the laundromat talking to the man who fills the snack machines. I asked him who you were. He couldn't remember your last name."

"Why did you want to know my name?"

"Because you look like an interesting person. How come I haven't seen you at school?"

"We just moved here in May." This was a truly astonishing conversation. She thought I looked interesting? "The only person I know besides Elliott is Paul Crowser."

Heather made a face. "That's not much of a recommendation. But I suppose he'll tell you all about me. Him and sweet sister, Vanessa."

"I guess you don't like them." Brilliant, Win. Why would she?

"Not much. But he's your friend, so I'll shut up. Let's talk about Elliott M. Deerfield. Now he sounds utterly fantastic."

"He is. You should see his house! It's like a museum. And there's hardly anything that man doesn't know something about, or any place he hasn't been."

I'd tell her about the opera. But not yet. She was still going through the magazines, laying the ones she wanted in a pile and putting the rest back in the boxes in order by month.

Then she stood up, and I couldn't *not* notice her enormous breasts again. I tried not to look at her. What are you supposed to do when somebody has something really obvious and you don't want to stare but all you can do is stare? Paul and his buddies were making sucking motions with their mouths. My face went red; I could feel it. I wished she'd leave.

"How much do I owe you?"

I was so embarrassed I could hardly add it up. She handed me four dollars and I gave her a quarter back.

"See you, Win." She looked at me with her serious eyes as though she expected me to say something.

"Yeah," I said. "See you, Heather."

She walked out of the yard without looking around, holding the sheaf of magazines against her chest.

"Hoooo boy!" Paul cackled. "Ever see such a pair of tits, Kelly? Those things should be on a cow, not on a girl! She could knock you unconscious if she ever turned around too fast, right, Steve?"

Heather must have heard every word he said.

Jamie, a jerk in a Harvard tee shirt, agreed with him. "Wouldn't mind milking them, though!" And he went *suck suck suck.*

"She's a tramp," Vanessa announced.

"How do you know?"

"Anybody with boobs like that has got to be a tramp. I mean, what else does she have to think about?"

"That doesn't make sense, Vanessa," I said.

"Does to me."

Vanessa had very small breasts, in fact hardly any at all. Because I was a coward, I didn't mention that.

We were pretty busy for the rest of the day, and I kept as far as possible from Paul and Vanessa. Most of the stuff was sold, but we still had Elliott's magazines, minus the ones Heather bought. I lugged the cartons into my room. Maybe I could find out where Heather lived and give them all to her, if Elliott didn't want them back. I began to daydream about seeing her at the laundromat. In the daydream we'd talk a little, and I'd tell her I had these magazines to give her, and then I'd go to her house with the boxes and we'd talk some more. Two cartons, two visits.

Finally Paul swaggered over to where I was going through the cash box. "Oh, Kelly, you were amazing! First you get connected with a fag, and the next thing I know you're hanging out with a whore with humongous tits."

And I blew up. "You know what? I may be amazing, but you're plain stupid. First of all, Elliott is no fag, you got that? That's just your idea about it. And second, Heather is not a whore. She's got a big . . . chest . . . but that doesn't mean she does anything bad."

"Everybody knows girls with big gazongas are easy. You can get them to have sex much quicker than the tiny-titted ones."

"You know that from personal experience, Crowser?"

"Let's just say I *know*." Smirking.

Probably the guys he hung out with told him that, but I doubted they knew any more than he did. As far as Paul was concerned, a man who liked opera and cooking was gay, and a girl with big breasts liked sex. It was that simple.

"I'm not putting up with any more of your crap," I yelled, and I ran into the house and slammed the door so hard the windows rattled.

# ELEVEN
## GENIUS

"Too wet," Elliott said Sunday afternoon. "We'll do the sculpture garden some other time. Let's bake bread."

He had everything lined up on the kitchen counter, the bowls, the baking pans, all the ingredients. He read the recipe aloud, explaining each step, and I measured and mixed.

"*Dissolve yeast in warm water.* Yeast is a living organism, like a plant. If the water is too hot, it kills the yeast. If it's too cold, nothing will happen." I checked the water temperature on my arm; not too hot, not too cold. "*Add spoonful of sugar.* The sugar feeds the yeast, like fertilizer, and the yeast produces carbon dioxide to make the dough rise." Bubbles formed in the bowl, just as Elliott predicted. "*Mix in flour using the hands. Turn dough out on lightly floured board and knead until elastic."* Elliott demonstrated kneading. Then I took over, folding and turning the warm dough. I caught on to that pretty quick.

"I knew you'd like this part," Elliott said. "It's good for the bread. Helps develop the gluten, part of the wheat flour that makes the dough stretchy. *Round up dough in greased bowl."*

While we waited for the dough to rise twice in the greased bowl and once in the pans, and finally to bake, we played chess. Another first for me.

Elliott set up the wooden chess board on the kitchen table, next to the open window. Rain was falling lightly; you could smell the wetness. He handed me the pieces one at a time, each piece a pottery sculpture glazed in black or white and decorated with bright colors. Each pawn was a different kind of tree. The knights were dragons, not horses' heads, the rooks really did look like miniature castles with tiny turrets and drawbridges, the bishops were represented by cathedrals. The queen was a young girl wearing a wreath of flowers in her long hair, and the king was the most wonderful of all: a unicorn with a shining silver horn.

"It's beautiful," I said, carefully setting the pieces where Elliott showed me. The queen with the wreath of flowers reminded me of Heather. I remembered what happened to the Irish glass, and I was afraid to touch them.

"Yes. Almost *too* beautiful. Sometimes it's hard not to get so caught up in the pieces that you lose your concentration on the game. If that happens we'll put this one away and get out the regular Staunton set."

I could see that the queen might cause me to lose my concentration, but I paid attention while Elliott explained each piece and how it moved: rook straight ahead or sideways, bishop on the diagonal, and most interesting of all, the knight that seemed to go around corners. You really had to keep your eye on that knight.

"The goal is simple," Elliott said. "To trap your opponent's king, the unicorn. The methods, however, are subtle. To begin with, the king is actually a very weak fellow. He can move only one square at a time, unlike the bishop, for instance, or the rook, which can race across the board. But trapping my king without losing your own turns out to be a very complicated business. You'll see."

For a few minutes nothing much happened, just my pawns marching toward Elliott's. "Remember how the bishop moves?"

"Diagonally."

"Look at my bishops. See anything one of them can do?"

I studied the situation. It was all a jumble to me. "I don't see anything."

Boom, there went my knight.

Once in a while I got lucky and took one of Elliott's pieces, but either it wasn't an important piece, or it set me up to lose another one of mine. Meanwhile the dough rose slowly and the rain splashed on the brick patio and Elliott talked.

He talked about Bobby Fischer, a genius who was an international grand master of chess at the age of fifteen, the youngest in history, and the youngest United States chess champion ever. Then he lectured on the subject of geniuses in general, and what genius is and why it isn't as important as hard work.

"That's not merely an Elliott Deerfield opinion.

Thomas Edison claimed that genius is actually a matter of one percent inspiration and ninety-nine percent perspiration." He interrupted himself. "Which reminds me—"

He went to the living room and turned on the stereo. "That's the overture to *The Magic Flute*," he said, sitting down again. "I want you to get used to hearing this music, so it will become familiar. If we play it every time you're here, it will gradually soak into your bones. There might even be a slight residue by Thursday. The big night, you know."

The last thing I wanted in my bones was an opera, and I did not want to be reminded of Thursday. While I was supposed to concentrate on the chess game and check on the rising dough, plus listen to the music, Elliott fed me little bits of information about Wolfgang Amadeus Mozart, who wrote *The Magic Flute*. By the time Mozart was thirteen he had composed a whole stack of music, symphonies and concertos and I don't know what else. I got the point: if Mozart could write all that music while he was still a kid, the least I could do was listen to it.

"Are you a genius, Elliott?"

"Heavens, no! Above average in intelligence, just as you are."

*What*? "You think I'm above average in intelligence?"

"Of course."

"But I don't do good in school."

"You don't do *well* in school. *Well* is an adverb, modifying the verb *to do*. *Good* is an adjective, and adjectives modify nouns. Hasn't anyone taught you the difference between an adverb and an adjective?"

"Probably." I shrugged. "I just don't remember. It's boring, all that grammar stuff."

"Now that," said Elliott, shaking his finger, "is why you don't do *well* in school. You decide that something is boring and you won't work at it. Back to Thomas Edison and his perspiration versus inspiration idea. If something doesn't inspire you, you don't want to sweat over it. Am I right?"

"Yeah."

"That doesn't mean that you're not smart, Win. Just undisciplined."

"You mean lazy."

"Laziness is a character defect. Lack of discipline is merely a bad habit. And habits can be corrected."

I almost told him then about wanting to be a writer; I was getting up my courage to say I sometimes thought about it, but he was off in another direction. He hauled out the old yellow pad and said, "Let's make a list of all the things you do and do not like to eat."

I did not want to make lists of food. I wanted to eat. But I humored him. "Salad. I don't like lettuce or any kind of raw vegetables."

He wrote it down. "What about cooked vegetables?"

"Nothing green, except sometimes peas."

"But you like vegetables if they're not green? Cauliflower, squash, carrots, mushrooms, onions, tomatoes?"

That was a trick question. "Carrots are okay sometimes. And corn. I like corn on the cob. And tomatoes only if they've been squished up in spaghetti sauce so there's no lumps."

He started a second column. "The only things I

have on the *Do Like* list are carrots, peas, and corn. That's not much of a list. How does your mother cook for you?"

"She never makes that kind of stuff anyway."

"What about fruits?"

"I like bananas, applesauce, and strawberries."

"That's all? Meat?"

"Any kind of meat except lamb, but I don't like fish except tuna. And shrimp cocktail."

"I'm surprised you haven't starved to death, or at least developed signs of malnutrition."

"I don't see what's so hard. I like lots of things."

He shoved the pad and pen across the table. "Here. Why don't you figure out some menus while I start lunch. I think I've got that one worked out, at least."

When we lived in Durango, the newspaper ran a weekly "School Menus" column that went like this: "Juicy meat patty on toasted bun with melted golden cheese and crunchy pickle garnish, fresh garden salad with creamy dressing, fruit jubilee and cookie." That translated as overcooked burger with plastic cheese and limp pickle, dead lettuce and brownish carrots, canned fruit cocktail embalmed in Jell-O. Everybody ate the burger and the cookie and left the rest. But at least I knew how a menu was supposed to sound.

"I'll tell you what we're having," Elliott said. "It's a *croque*. *Croque Monsieur* is French for a toasted ham and cheese sandwich." He printed it on the pad. It looked funny, but he pronounced it "Croak M'Sure." "But since I don't have any good smoked ham I'll substitute green chili. Maybe we should call it '*Croque Santa Fe*.' There's also the *Croque Madame*, which substitutes sliced mushrooms for the ham, and *Croque Vivienne*, made with veal."

This was how we made melted cheese sandwiches at home: Slap a couple of American single slices between two pieces of white bread and fry until bread is toasted and cheese is melted, which if you do it right happens at the same time. If you don't, the bread burns and the cheese stays stiff and cold.

But this was how Elliott did it: Cut slices from a loaf of homemade bread (not the one that had just gone in the oven) and Swiss cheese from a big wedge (the kind with small holes, not big ones); put them on one slice of bread; add long strips of green chili; cover with second slice; dip sandwiches in eggs beaten with cream, and fry slowly in butter. And that was his new invention, *Croque Santa Fe*.

"Usually I'd serve this with broiled herbed tomatoes and a tossed green salad, but in your case"— he had his head in the refrigerator—" we'll make that carrot salad."

I was all set to hate the carrot salad. But this was not like any school menu Crunchy Carrot Medley with canned pineapple and raisins. These were cold cooked carrots in herb dressing with peas and sliced egg scattered on top. This would be my fourth meal with Elliott, counting the good one in the restaurant where we ate burgers. I was getting so I could stand it.

"How is it?"

"Not bad."

"Next time we'll make spaghetti. From scratch."

"Sounds good."

It sounded more than just good. I'd show Paul there was nothing weird, queer, or faggotish about eating good food, and nothing weird, queer, or faggotish about cooking it either. I'd fix him a lunch like this. But then I remembered the things he had said about Heather, and I decided he could just as well starve.

# TWELVE

## THE UNICORN UNIFORM

"I suppose you think I ought to wear a tuxedo."

"It might be fun," Ma said, talking loud over the *cluckcluckcluck* of the sewing machine. It sounded like a hen laying an egg. Ma was fixing another batch of worn-out jeans. You'd be surprised at the condition of some of the pants people expected her to patch—not just the knees but sometimes the whole crotch gone or the seat worn out. "Did you discuss it with Elliott? How does *he* dress to go to the opera?"

"He said a nice shirt would be fine, except I don't even have a nice shirt. And I'm supposed to wear something warm, because it gets really cold up there. But I don't have a jacket either, anyway not a nice one. Maybe I shouldn't go at all, huh? I don't want to embarrass him in front of his friends."

"You'd just love to get out of this, wouldn't you? But I'm not going to let you. It's a once-in-a-lifetime experience. I'll go over to Tia Maria's Thrift Shop tomorrow and see what they've got."

Now this was typical of the way my mother did things. She wouldn't go out and buy Donny or me or herself something from an ordinary store. No, she had to dig around in second-hand shops and the Salvation Army and church rummage sales, and she'd find stuff that might have been all right twenty years ago when it was new. She'd get excited about the cloth it was made out of or the way it was sewed, sometimes she'd go berserk over *buttons*, and she'd bring it home and say she was going to do something with it. All it needed was about eight hours of work, but she never found the eight hours.

It was like the broken-down furniture she collected and which we had finally gotten rid of at the yard sale: great a long time ago, maybe it could be again, but it never got done. She said she had turned over a new leaf, but I knew it was just a matter of time until the place started filling up again with "treasures." Probably a good thing, because at that point we had almost nothing to sit on.

At Tia Maria's she found a pair of gray pants that were too long, a white shirt that needed ironing, and a gray and blue striped tie that wasn't too ugly except I hate neckties. "I'm sorry, but I couldn't find a decent jacket."

"It's okay," I said. Maybe if I didn't have a jacket I wouldn't have to go. Elliott wouldn't want me to catch cold.

"I have an idea, though," she said and went back

to her bedroom. She brought out the jacket she had made for Bobby Don with unicorns embroidered on the front and back. I was surprised to see it; I thought he had taken it with him. It was wrinkled but still beautiful.

"I've been saving this for Donny, but you can wear it in the meantime. Try it on."

"It's going to be too big."

"You don't know that yet." She held it out to me with a shake. "Here, take it."

"How come he left it here? See, it's too big."

"He never liked it that much. It wasn't *macho* enough, I guess. It's not *that* much too big. You can turn up the cuffs. That leaves room for a sweater. I have one you can wear."

"I'm not going to wear your sweater!"

"Who's going to know it's mine? It's that navy blue one with the crew neck. It'll look nice with the shirt and pants."

Quite an outfit. At least it wasn't a tuxedo.

Ma had gotten as far as pinning up the cuffs of the pants. The unicorn jacket was still a wrinkled mess. I plugged in the iron to press the jacket and went to work on the pants. I hated sewing with a needle and thread, but Ma had showed me how to run her machine. She promised to teach me to mend jeans if I wanted to learn, and I could do things that weren't too complicated and be paid for it. She never got around to teaching me exactly how to do it, but I knew enough to hem a couple of pantlegs.

Which is what I was doing when Paul walked in. I didn't hear him. I looked up and there he was.

"Making something sweet to wear to the opera tonight, Winston?" he said in this pukey voice he put on whenever he was working me over about Elliott. "I thought maybe your fairy godfather would touch you with his magic wand and presto! Satin tights."

"Funny. You're always so funny. I'm just trying to shorten these pants because Ma doesn't have time to do it."

"Surrrrrre, Win."

"You don't think I'd be doing this if I didn't have to, do you?"

"I think it's very sweet that you can sew."

"Look, sewing isn't something just for girls to do. It's useful and practical, like cooking. Ma says a man needs to be able to take care of himself, just like a woman needs to be able to take care of herself, because you never know what's going to happen in this life."

Paul flopped down on the floor. There was no place to sit now that the saggy sofa was gone. "What does your mother do to take care of herself?"

"She fixes things. Like when her bicycle has a flat tire, she doesn't have to get some man to fix it for her. And she can build things. Don't you remember our house in Durango when she built a whole greenhouse on one side of it?"

"Bobby Don did that."

Now I was getting mad. "Bobby Don didn't do *nothing*. I mean, anything. Ma did it all, except pour the concrete. Bobby Don was gone when she did that greenhouse. You don't remember anything right, do you?"

But remembering right made me mad at Bobby Don, too. I wasn't sure I wanted to wear his unicorn jacket after all. How come he didn't like it enough to take it with him when he left?

Paul pulled on his lower lip in the way he had when he was about to say something nasty. "So why doesn't she fix stuff around here? The whole place looks like it's falling down."

"Because she doesn't have time, dummy. Because she's got three jobs and she goes to school besides." I was getting hot. "And what about *your* mother? Can she fix anything?"

"She doesn't have to. She has a good job. She gets lots of tips from those old ladies who come into the beauty shop to get their hair permed and dyed, so when something around our place breaks down she just calls somebody up and pays them to come and repair it. Simple."

"That's what we'll do when Ma finishes school and gets a job in an office. We'll have plenty of money then." I went to work on the unicorn jacket, ironing it on the wrong side the way Ma showed me to protect the embroidery. Paul watched.

"I'm going to Dallas," Paul said after a while. "This afternoon."

"So your mom gave in and said you could go?"

"Yeah, she said it's my funeral. I have no one to blame but myself, not to come crying to her, and so on and so forth."

"You'll do okay. When are you coming back?"

"Couple of weeks, I guess." He licked his lips and rubbed his eyes. "Dad's taking off a week from work. He sells cars for a Mercedes dealer now, did I tell you that? And he drives a Mercedes himself, a 450 SL.

He's going to pick me up at the airport in it. And we're going to go all kinds of places, Six Flags which is like an amusement park, and I don't know where all." I unplugged the iron and folded up the ironing board. "It's real hot in Dallas now. I sure do hope he's got air conditioning." As though that was the thing he worried about most.

"I'll walk you to the airport bus." He was still my friend, after all.

He had on a shirt and jacket, the first I had seen him out of army fatigues in weeks, and he had a fresh haircut. He was excited and talked too fast, jumping from one subject to another. He kept running a hand over his haircut, as though he was making sure it was still there.

"What time does the fun begin?" he asked.

I hoped the Dallas trip would make him forget about the opera, but it didn't. "Elliott's picking me up at five-thirty. We're meeting some friends of his, Dr. Vogel and Dr. Vogel, to eat first."

"Dr. Vogel and Dr. Vogel? Your needle stuck or what?"

"They're both doctors of some kind."

We saw the bus turn the corner. I was glad he was leaving.

"Have a good time in Dallas," I said. "Take it easy."

He climbed on and found a seat in the back. Sliding open the tinted window he called out to me, "You have a good time at the opera. Don't forget the perfume behind your ears."

* * *

At a quarter of five Ma raced up on her bicycle. I was already dressed, except that I didn't know how to tie a necktie, and she didn't either.

"Ask Elliott to tie it for you," she said. "I'm sure he'll know how. Put on the jacket and let's see how you look."

It was too big, but with the sleeves turned up it was still a great jacket. Now the only problem was shoes. We forgot about shoes. All I had was sneakers, and they weren't in such great shape.

"Don't worry about them. There's no sense worrying about things you can't do anything about"— Ma's usual advice—"and with Elliott coming in ten minutes, there's nothing you can do. If you don't let it bother you, I'm sure it won't bother anyone else."

"It bothers me."

"Oh Win, if you only realized how handsome you look, you wouldn't think another thing about your feet!"

"I'll concentrate on being handsome from the ankles up."

Elliott arrived looking like something out of *Gentleman's Quarterly*. He wasn't wearing a tie but had some kind of maroon silk scarf inside the collar of his shirt, which was unbuttoned at the top. Ma went up to him and felt the sleeve of his jacket. It was the color of gingerale, the kind of cloth you wanted to touch, but I was embarrassed that she did it.

"Raw silk," she said.

"I've had it for years. Bought it in Hong Kong on my first trip to China." He turned to me. "My but don't you look stink elegant!"

I turned red. *Stink elegant?* Was that good? "Can you help me tie my tie?"

"Let's do it in front of a mirror," he said. "That way you'll see how to do it yourself."

Elliott loomed above me by a head in the bathroom mirror. While we were going right-over-left, Donny came in from playing and peed, staring up at Elliott and not looking what he was doing. "Will you teach me someday too, Elliott?"

"Of course."

"Right now?"

"No, but the next time I'm here."

Donny stomped out. "Flush!" I yelled after him. Donny still hadn't gotten an amigo, and he acted up every time I did something with Elliott. No matter what it was, he'd start pestering. The only thing he hadn't pestered about was going to the opera.

"All set?" Elliott asked. Ma followed us out to the car with a big proud smile on her face, as though I had just graduated from something.

"It'll be very late when we get back, Laurel," Elliott said. "Probably one-thirty or so."

She said she didn't mind at all. "Be good," she said to me. "Have fun!" she told us both.

Fat chance.

# THIRTEEN

## THE GANGSTER &
## THE WITCH

**P**HIL AND SARA have invited us to eat dinner
at their place," Elliott said as we drove off, and I was
instantly nervous. I didn't like meeting people I didn't
know, although I guess the first time you meet people
you don't know them. And I didn't like going to a
stranger's house to eat. Probably they were gourmets
like Elliott and I'd have to choke down snails or squid
or something. I did not understand how people could
swallow things like oysters and clams. I thought about
the leftover pizza at home in the fridge. Donny would
demolish it before I got back.

Elliott must have been a mind reader. He said,
"Don't worry about this, Win. The Vogels are nice
people and they're looking forward to meeting you. It

was their idea that I sign up with Los Amigos, remember? They also got the extra ticket so you could go tonight."

I should have been grateful. I wasn't.

The Vogels lived in one of those big old adobe houses like the ones my mother cleaned, not like ours. Pink and white flowers filled the pots shaped liked animals parading along the portal. Dr. Vogel and Dr. Vogel both met us at the door. He was short and round and mostly bald and had a little mustache, and she was tall and thin with frizzy gray hair that stuck out all over her head. He looked like a gangster and she looked like a witch. They were dressed in matching Indian outfits made of brown velvet, and they both wore silver belts and silver necklaces decorated with chunks of turquoise.

There were paintings of Indians on all the walls and Indian baskets and Indian pots on the tables and Indian rugs on the floor and Indian blankets draped on the sofa and chairs. It looked like a trading post, and they looked like a couple of traders.

Elliott handed over a paper bag to Dr. Philip Vogel, who peered inside and said, "Two bottles of white Zinfandel and two cans of Dr Pepper. Thanks!" Good old Elliott.

They opened the wine and poured the soda into a wine glass and we settled down to play question-and-answer—the Vogels asking the questions and me answering—about where I lived and where I used to live, and about my parents and Donny and so forth, the usual kind of questions adults always ask. "Now you ask us questions," Dr. Philip Vogel said.

"It's only fair," Dr. Sara Vogel said. "We've been grilling you and now it's your turn. What would you like to know about us?"

Since this never happens I couldn't think of a single question. "Why don't you ask them about their work?" Elliott suggested. He was sitting next to me on the sofa; the Vogels had taken their places in two matching La-Z-Boy recliners with their feet up, and they were sipping wine, very relaxed. I wondered why Dr. Sara Vogel wasn't out in the kitchen getting the food ready. I couldn't smell anything cooking, which probably meant we were having gazpacho and chicken salad, if not something worse.

"That's a good idea," I said. "Where do you work?" From the look of things it must have been on an Indian reservation.

"We're both psychologists," Dr. Sara said. "We're in practice together."

"In the phone book it says Dr. Sara Vogel in big black letters, and right underneath it it says Dr. Philip Vogel in little tiny letters. That's because she's bigger than I am. Strong as an ox. She wins all the battles. And if she says, 'Your name is going to be in teeny weeny type below mine,' then that's how it is. No argument."

"It's not because I'm bigger, it's because I'm smarter."

"That's right," Dr. Philip said, nodding his head seriously. "And she's also older. Sara is years and years older than I am. She practically stole me right out of my playpen."

"Cage," she said. "I stole him out of his cage. I thought he'd make a nice house pet."

"She's still trying to housebreak me. Did you notice the newspapers all over the kitchen floor?"

I never heard two adults talk like that to each other. It had to be a joke. They never smiled or changed expression, but they didn't get mad either. I turned around to Elliott, who just winked at me. Then the doorbell rang.

"There's dinner," Philip said.

Nobody moved. The doorbell rang again. "Coming!" Dr. Sara called, but she stayed in her chair and smiled at Philip.

Philip made a face as though his ear hurt. "She's got a louder voice than mine, too." He crawled out of his recliner and went to the door. He came back carrying two big flat boxes. Pizza? Were we really going to have pizza?

"Dinner's served," Dr. Sara said, finally getting up, and we all trooped into the dining room after Dr. Philip with the two boxes.

There were four places set at the dining room table, with china plates and silver. Philip poured the second Dr Pepper into my wine glass, and Dr. Sara ripped the tops off the boxes. And there were two pizzas such as I have never seen in my life, like paintings of some fantastic underwater scene. I couldn't tell what any of the stuff on them was, couldn't spot the mushrooms or anchovies.

"PizzArt," Dr. Sara said. "Aren't they pretty? Some day I'm going to spray one with plastic and hang it on my office wall."

"One of your patients would eat it. I can think of several who might," Dr. Philip said. "Plastic and all."

"The fellow who does it is a painter who wasn't getting anywhere with his oils," Dr. Sara explained. "The galleries wouldn't hang them. So he started making pizzas and managed to get one of the big gallery owners to serve them at the opening of a new exhibit. When the newspaper reviewer wrote up the show, he made a big fuss over the PizzArt and hardly mentioned the watercolors or whatever it was."

"And suddenly the artist—his name is Mike something but he calls himself Miguel—is in demand for big parties, and he opened a shop called Edible Collages."

"I hear he's making a fortune," Dr. Sara said. "You never have the slightest idea what you're eating, but it looks gorgeous and it does *taste* Italian. So dig in. Win? Can I serve you a piece?"

It seemed too bad to cut the thing up, but Elliott was already working on a slice, raving about the fresh herbs. The only resemblance it had to regular pizza was that it was round and flat with dough on the bottom, but from there on it was all different. If I was going to try to sift out the onion and who knows what else was buried there, I'd probably end up with nothing but naked dough. I decided I better get on with it.

I don't know what I ate, but it was delicious.

Elliott is not a person who enjoys his food in silence. He likes to talk about what he's eating the whole time he's eating it, so it was prosciutto this and pesto that. I had a second slice, and then two more. The rest of them were finished, and I was still stuffing my face.

"*Mahvelous* dinner, my love," said Dr. Philip Vogel, in a fake British accent.

"*Thenk yaw, dahling,*" said Dr. Sara Vogel.

"Isn't she a wonderful cook, Win? A real tiger in the kitchen. Did you see the way she ripped the tops off the boxes? RRRRRRRrrrr."

These two kidded all the time, like characters on a TV sit com. I said, "It was real good, *thenk yaw*." And they all laughed at my fake British accent.

Next came dessert. Popsicles.

Dr. Sara carried in a silver tray with seven popsicles arranged like spokes on a wheel. "You each can have two. I'm dieting." Which seemed strange to me, because Dr. Philip was the fat one who should have been eating less. Dr. Sara was skinny as a pole. We sucked on our popsicles until Elliott announced that we'd better get going if we wanted to find a reasonable place to park.

I put on my unicorn jacket, and Dr. Sara went crazy over it. She twirled me around so she could study it and peeled it off me to look at the wrong side of the stitches.

"Absolutely gorgeous," Dr. Sara Vogel pronounced. "Philip, look at this and tell me if it isn't the most gorgeous jacket you've ever seen in your life."

"It is the most gorgeous jacket I've ever seen in my life," Dr. Philip repeated, in a flat voice like a memorized speech, but he winked at me.

"Your mother made it, Win?" Dr. Sara demanded.

"Yes."

"This woman has talent."

"You bet she has talent," Elliott said. "I just bought some sketches of hers and framed them. Great strength, great simplicity. And the amazing thing is, I don't think she knows how good she is."

"She doesn't," I agreed.

"Well, we'll have to do something about *that*," Dr. Sara declared in a voice you'd never argue with. "I know plenty of people who'd love to own something like this."

We piled into the Vogels' black and tan Rolls Royce with deep leather seats and little vases of flowers. Dr. Philip peered up over the steering wheel, Dr. Sara sat straight as a duchess beside him, and Elliott and I lounged in the back seat like a couple of celebrities, rock stars, or Arab oil sheiks. I could sure give Paul an earful about all of this, the PizzArt and popsicles, the Vogels and the Rolls. Eat your heart out, Paul Crowser, I thought.

But I was also thinking, I can't wait to tell Heather. I wouldn't leave out a thing.

# FOURTEEN
### •
# THE MAGIC ROLLS

**T**HE ROLLS SWEPT majestically up the curving driveway to the opera. Guys directing traffic stepped respectfully aside. Dr. Phil waved grandly and steered past them into the parking lot. He not so much *parked* the car as *abandoned* it, knowing I guess that nobody was going to mess with a car like that. We joined a crowd of people funneled toward the entrance gate like a flock of exotic birds, some dressed up in tuxedos and long dresses, some in jeans and backpacks.

The Santa Fe Opera was partly inside and partly outside. A roof came out over the stage and another roof covered the balcony, but the two didn't meet. The space between was open, and you could see the sky.

Everywhere we went there were people who knew Elliott and Dr. Sara and Dr. Philip, and there was a lot of hand-shaking and introducing going on: "I'd like you to meet my friend, Win Kelly." How do you do, shake hands, nice to meet you, and so on.

"So this is Vin!" said a woman with a German accent, grabbing Elliott's arm. She had dyed red hair and came only partway up to Elliott's shoulder. "Ve haf zeartinly heard a great deal about you."

"You have?"

"Oh ja, ja, all of it fery, fery goot, of course." She jabbed his chest with her finger and said, "Don't keep this luffly boy a secret," and walked away.

*Luffly boy?* That's the kind of thing Paul Crowser would laugh himself sick over.

We found our seats in the open part where there was no roof and began to look over our programs. Everyone settled down and the lights dimmed and the orchestra rose up out of somewhere and started to play. "The overture," Elliott whispered. I recognized the music, which had been soaking into my bones for weeks.

Out came the prince, Tamino, chased by a fake-looking serpent. Three ladies dressed alike killed the serpent, but not until they sang about it. Next came Papageno, a chubby fellow dressed in feathers who was a born liar and ended up with a padlock on his mouth. The Queen of the Night swooped up dramatically ("She's on a hydraulic lift," Elliott said) all in black and silver and singing in a huge voice full of throb and thrill. ("God, she's marvelous!" Elliott breathed, and I kind of had to agree with him). The Queen's daughter was named Pamina, and you could tell from her name that she'd end up with Tamino by the end of the story.

Tamino got a magic flute, which could change people's passions, and Papageno, the porkchop in feathers, had some kind of chiming bells. Tamino tootled his flute and forest animals tumbled onto the stage, played by kids in animal suits who sang in those thin silvery voices like the boys in white smocks on television around Christmas time. I wondered where they got the kids who would do this.

Sarastro was Pamina's father. The Queen of the Night hated him, but somebody named Monostatos seemed to be the villain, although I didn't think much of Sarastro either as far as that went. I couldn't tell which side the Queen was on. There were all kinds of tests that the prince had to go through, and Papageno was singing away with Pamina and wishing he had a girl of his own, a Papagena.

Elliott and I had been through all of this in the synopsis, and so I knew the names when they came out on stage and Elliott told me who was who, but I couldn't remember what was going on and Elliott said not to worry, it didn't make much difference anyway, the music was the important thing.

The first rumble of thunder sounded like a drum-beat during something the Queen was pumping out full throttle, and a bolt of lightning ripped the sky to the west. Nobody paid the slightest attention. The thunder rolled in closer and the lightning circled all around us. The first drops of rain splashed down before anybody stirred. I wondered if we were going to run for it or what. Without taking his eyes off the stage, Elliott groped in a small bag he had been carrying and pulled out a couple of plastic ponchos. I dived into the one he

gave me, pulling the hood up over my head. The
Vogels struggled into matching yellow foul-weather
suits. They looked as though they should have been at
the helm of a schooner during a tropical typhoon.

By then the rain was coming down in torrents.
People in the other uncovered seats were also putting
up or popping open umbrellas. A few got up and moved
back to stand in the shelter of the balcony. I thought
we'd do that too; I should have known better. I
huddled under a tent of blue plastic, but Dr. Vogel
and Dr. Vogel sat like a couple of cheerful ducks, one
tall and skinny, one short and broad, while the rain
poured down over them.

Up on stage the singers were warm and dry and
kept right on singing at the tops of their lungs over the
drumrolls of thunder and pelting rain, the scenery
changed, the orchestra sawed away, and the mystery
of the plot got thicker and thicker.

At intermission we went to drain off. The rain
had let up, but it was cold. I was glad I had the unicorn
jacket under the poncho but was wishing I had remembered to bring Ma's sweater. We joined the crowd
around the refreshment stand, and Elliott bought me
a hot chocolate.

"Well, Win, what do you think?"

I held the plastic cup in both hands, trying to
soak up some warmth. "It's good," I said, which was
only half a lie. "I'm enjoying it." Also half.

Dr. Sara watched me with a little smile. When
Elliott turned around to talk to someone else, she
whispered, "Why don't you just admit that you're
bored out of your tree?"

"Because it would hurt Elliott's feelings," I said, and that was the whole truth.

"You're right," she said. "But until you came along I wouldn't have thought Elliott Deerfield had any feelings to hurt. He's very fond of you, you know."

"Yeah," I said, feeling uncomfortable.

"You're very good for him, and I imagine he's good for you, too. Am I right?"

"Yeah." I grabbed a fast look at her and stared at the ends of my worn-out sneakers. The Big Question was whirring through my head again.

"They're signaling for the next act," Elliott said. "Where's Philip?"

"He went to the car."

Dr. Sara and Elliott and I returned to our seats. No Dr. Phil. The rain had stopped and rainwater was draining out through the holes drilled in the seats of the chairs. We stayed wrapped in our ponchos to keep warm.

A couple more hours of singing and flashing and booming with everything working out fine for everybody, people paired off the way they should be, and it was over. The seat next to Dr. Sara stayed empty. Elliott was on his feet applauding and yelling "Bravo!" Almost everybody else was doing it, so I stood up and clapped and yelled "Bravo" too, but not as loud as Elliott. We joined the mob on the way to the car, which was easy to spot because there weren't many Rolls Royces in the parking lot.

Dr. Philip was curled up in the back seat, sound asleep. Dr. Sara woke him and got him to sit up so I could climb in next to him. Elliott sat in front with Dr.

Sara, who drove us majestically back to town while Dr. Philip, asleep again, snored loudly. I must have dozed off too, because the next thing I knew I was in front of my house, and Elliott was shaking me. I woke up enough to crawl out of the car, mumble thank you to Dr. Sara and Elliott, and stumble into the house and into bed.

The opera was over, and I had survived. What made me mad was that it was so late when we got back that nobody saw me being delivered to my home in a Rolls Royce, a thing that might never happen again.

# FIFTEEN

## HUCK & WIN

Y AAIIIYEEEEE!
I froze by the door and listened; it happened again, the yell from somewhere upstairs, in Elliott's office. He's really gone off, I thought, and rang the doorbell; maybe he's taken up opera singing. I hadn't seen him since the night of *The Magic Flute* and the Rolls Royce.

He came to the door in black pajamas with a purple sash around his waist. He was barefoot, and little channels of sweat zigzagged down his neck. "Hi, Win," he said, breathless but cheery. "I was just practicing my kung fu."

"Kung fu?" I repeated. "You're doing kung fu?"

"I thought I told you about that. I've been at it for several months now. I'm enjoying it a great deal."

I had never known anybody like Elliott for jumping into weirdness and enjoying it a great deal.

"I'm sorry I'm not ready," Elliott said, "but I wanted to work through another *kata*."

"*Kata?*" My brilliant conversation seemed to be limited to repeating whatever Elliott said.

"A *kata* is a sequence of movements. The movements are called 'weapons,' but when you put them together so that they flow into one another, it's like a dance, very choreographic. Want to see one?"

"Sure."

"Come on up to my office. I work out there because there's more space."

I followed him up the narrow circular staircase, and he pointed for me to sit in his desk chair. Elliott bowed to me and began to move in the most amazing ways, leaping and twisting, his body weaving and arcing. He bowed again when he finished and sat down on the floor. "What do you think?"

"It looks great."

"It all has to do with balance," he said, and he was off on another tear, explaining the philosophy of kung fu, a martial art from China. So far he had worked through white, orange, and purple belts. "The colors of the belts represent levels of achievement, a Western innovation," he explained, "because we're so goal-oriented in this culture and have to be rewarded each step of the way." Soon he would be evaluated for his blue belt. After that came green and three degrees of brown. The black belt was the highest level, and there were eight degrees; his instructor, Jack Mooney, had attained his sixth.

"Some day I'll take you to meet Jack," Elliott said, mopping his face with a towel. "He's quite a character to talk to, but when he moves, it's pure poetry. Maybe,"

Elliott said, cocking an eyebrow, "you'd be interested in lessons."

"Not me," I said. "You can get hurt with that stuff."

"Not the way Jack teaches. He stresses internal attitudes, creating the circumstances, taking charge of the situation. If you need to use the "weapons" out on the street, then you're not interested in balance and interaction; you're out to win, to subdue your opponent. But in class we're not winning, we're working in harmony with a partner. There are women in my class. Boys your age, too."

"No thanks."

"I'll take you to meet Jack anyway." Elliott does not give up easily. "Listen, I promised you a movie, didn't I? Let me jump in the shower, and I'll be ready in five minutes. Ten at the most. We'll come back here after the movie to eat. I'm leaving at five o'clock tomorrow morning on a business trip, and I haven't even started to pack yet."

"I didn't know you were going away."

"Just for a couple of weeks in New York and Washington." He started downstairs. "Why don't you stay up here and take a look around? See if you notice anything different," he said, grinning back at me.

I wandered around the office and peered through the telescope at the mountain, which still had a patch of snow at the top. The computer was covered with a brown nylon jacket; some day maybe Elliott would let me fool with it. Low bookshelves along the walls where the sloping ceiling cut in were filled with scientific books and technical magazines. A stack of *Smithsonians* reminded me of Heather.

On the wall next to the stairwell I discovered what was different: Ma's sketches hung in two rows, four above, four below. He had mounted them on dark blue board just as they were torn out of the sketch book, leaving the ragged edge, and framed them in shiny aluminum. I thought they looked good in the sketchbook, but hung on a wall, like real art, they looked wonderful. I examined one of a baby sucking its thumb and realized it must have been Donny. She hadn't done any artwork since then.

Elliott's damp head appeared over the edge of the stairwell. He was grinning again.

"Like them?"

"I wish Ma could see them. Maybe she'd see how good she is."

"Excellent idea. When I come back we'll have the whole family over for dinner and an art show. You can do the cooking. Now we're going to have to move fast to make the movie on time."

It was French—okay, but not great. Elliott went into a frenzy over it, as usual. The dinner was spaghetti with mussels. I tried to avoid the mussels until I saw the look on Elliott's face and knew I was in for another lecture if I didn't swallow at least one. I eased a rubbery creature into my mouth; better than I expected. In fact I ate all he'd given me. Score a point for Elliott.

He packed for the trip as though he were putting together a machine. He stacked some shirts and hung a gray suit over a special hanger, rolled his socks in balls and fitted them in corners. "What are you going to do with yourself for the next week or so, Win?"

I said I didn't have any plans.

"Maybe you'd like to borrow some books."

"Like what?"

"Up to you. Let's go take a look."

There must have been hundreds of books on his living room shelves, and I had never heard of any of them until my eye lit on *Huckleberry Finn*. "I never read that one," I said.

"You haven't?" He sounded amazed. "I thought everybody had read *Huck Finn* at least once before sixth grade. I read it for the first time when I was eight and quite a few times since. But that's the TV generation for you, don't know any of the classics." He handed me the book.

We sat out on the portal and had a farewell wine and Dr Pepper. As I got ready to go home, *Huck Finn* under my arm, I said, "Goodbye, have a good trip," and Elliott put his arm around my shoulders and hugged me. He was the first person besides Ma who had hugged me for a long time, and it felt good. But on the way home I started to worry, that maybe liking Elliott to hug me meant there was something wrong with me. And still I didn't have anybody to talk to about this.

The first thing I noticed about *Huckleberry Finn* was the terrible grammar. Double negatives all over the place. Elliott must have noticed. I was surprised that the book was not all marked up with corrections, the way he did with grammar lessons on the yellow pad. It took me a while to get used to reading it, especially when Mark Twain got into the conversation of Jim, the black guy Huck went down the Mississippi with on the raft, which was all written in peculiar spellings.

I liked Huck right away, and I began to feel that

we had a good many things in common besides bad grammar, like not having a father (Huck's was terrible; that's why Huck ran away) and then finding a friend in the runaway slave Jim. Not that Elliott was anything like Jim. In fact you could say that they were exactly opposites, because Jim had no education at all and had to depend on Huck. Even though Huckleberry's grammar was miserable, he was the "educated" one who could read, and Jim couldn't. They took good care of each other. You might even say they loved each other.

Imagine going down a huge river on a raft and catching fish and shooting small game and birds and "borrowing" chickens and watermelons from people's gardens. I thought about how it would be to go on a voyage like that with Elliott, camping out on little islands, telling stories around a campfire at night, having adventures.

What if I wrote a book and told stories about Elliott and me and the things we did together—like going to the track and the kayak races and photographing wildflowers? I'd try to describe it just the way it sounded. I would not tell Elliott about it. I would just keep doing it until I had a book, and I'd call it *The Adventures of Elliott and Win*. I was crazy enough to do that.

# SIXTEEN

## • LONESOME

**D**ONNY WAS assembling flufferbanutters and had a whole stack of lumpy, gooey sandwiches.

"How come you're making all these?"

"We're going on a picnic. Hal's taking us. He'll be here pretty soon."

Donny finally had an amigo, Hal Norris. Hal was divorced and had one kid, Joey, who stayed with him all summer, and I guess he thought it would be good for Joey to have another kid to do things with. But Hal was a big jock and Joey was a little jock and Donny was a couch potato with two left feet.

The first time they went for a hike Donny came home crying because he had blisters on his heels. When they pitched softballs Donny came home crying because he bruised his thumb and they said he couldn't catch it right or throw it right. Joey was in Little

League, and Hal made it sound as though if you weren't in Little League you were probably not a real American. Totally different from Elliott, whose opinion of baseball ranked it right up there with watching paint dry.

Poor Donny. It bothered him more than it did me that his father wasn't around. Some day he'd probably want to find Bobby Don Willett the way I wanted to find Michael X. Kelly, the way Paul was trying to find out what kind of person his father was. But it was a dangerous business. I could guess what Donny would discover when he went looking for Bobby Don. I remembered him coming in drunk lots of times, but Donny was too young to remember that.

Donny wanted an amigo because I had one. But now he was having as much trouble with Hal as I had at first with Elliott, only in a different way: baseball instead of opera. Elliott had certain ideas of what an amigo should be, and I had other ideas. Now Hal wanted Donny to be an athlete and company for his kid, probably more than he wanted to be company for Donny. Sometimes I wondered if people ever stopped to figure out why they wanted to do something.

At least on a picnic Donny wasn't going to get any more blisters, unless the picnic was an excuse for a forced march. "How come you're making so many?"

"Because Ma isn't going to have time, and she told Hal we'd bring the sandwiches. So I have to fix them."

"Ma's going too?"

"Uh-huh."

"How come?"

"Cause Hal asked her to."

"He didn't ask me."

"You got an amigo and Ma doesn't. Hal's lots better than Elliott anyway," he said.

I was wrapping the fifth sticky sandwich when Ma rode up on her old bike, leaned it against the wall, and rushed into the house. "Hi, guys! I'm grabbing a quick shower!" she sang out and disappeared into the bathroom.

I checked the refrigerator to see what there was for my supper. Not much, as usual. "You going to let me have one of those?" I asked Donny.

"No. We gotta have lots of them."

I wondered how Hal felt about flufferbanutters. I could imagine Elliott's reaction if I served flufferbanutters on a picnic. He'd probably make a long speech on the evils of marshmallow, and that made me laugh and feel better about everybody going out.

Ma came into the kitchen in white pants and a new flowered shirt. She looked very pretty. "If I give you some money and a list," she said, fastening on long dangly earrings, "would you pick up some things at the supermarket? We're out of practically everything, as you probably noticed. You can take my bike."

Add riding my mother's bike to the list of things I hate. I also hated grocery shopping, almost as much as doing the laundry. But if I was going to eat, I didn't have much choice.

Ma and Donny were still getting ready for their picnic with Hal and Joey when I wheeled the bike out onto the street. Why hadn't they asked me to go along? It would have made more sense if Hal invited me instead of Ma, who wasn't even in the Amigo program.

The list was scribbled on the back of the gas bill:

*Cheese,* which meant packaged American slices. Ma always got that because it didn't dry out, and it was easy for Donny to handle. But I looked over the cheese section and found a chunk of Swiss, the kind Elliott bought, and I got that instead.

*Bread.* I passed up the regular sliced white like the flufferbanutter kind. They had something like Elliott's crunchy whole wheat kind in the bakery section. I dropped it in the shopping cart.

Eggs and milk were on the list, so I had everything I needed to make "croques." I intended to go home and fix myself the kind of supper Elliott would have cooked, the kind he probably ate when he was alone. I even bought some frozen carrots and peas and some dressing to soak them in to make myself a *salad.* And I tossed some yeast and flour in the cart, in case I decided to try to bake bread someday. If everybody was going on picnics or trips to Dallas and New York while I stayed home, I might as well learn to cook.

When I got to the checkout counter I saw Heather Key in line ahead of me. "Hi, Win," she said and gave me a big smile. Her eyes were the color of Rocky Mountain iris. My mouth went dry.

"Hi, how's it going?" Notice the suave reply. I couldn't think what to say to this girl.

"Fine. Those magazines I bought from you were really interesting."

"Good. I've still got the rest of them. You can have them if you want them."

"I can? That's very nice. How's Elliott M. Deerfield?"

"He's okay, I guess. He's away on business right now."

"I'd really like to meet him."

"I'll introduce you sometime." I tried to imagine what *that* would be like, me stumbling over names and messing up the whole thing. I started to babble. "My little brother just got an amigo, and he has to go on long hikes with him. Poor kid is going to be one big blister before the summer's over. Tonight they're on a picnic. My mother went along."

"Didn't you want to go?"

"I wasn't invited. So I'm going home and fix myself a gourmet dinner. Do you know what a croque monsieur is?"

"I never heard of it."

I blabbed on. I told her how I was going to make it, even the carrot and pea salad. I mentioned that I bought flour and yeast and was planning to start making all our bread. I even managed to tell her about gluten in the flour and carbon dioxide in the dough. It sounded like one of Elliott's lectures.

We both had our bags of groceries. I had to load mine into the baskets of my mother's bike.

"I'd really like to learn how to make bread," she said. She shuffled her bags, pushing up a sagging one with her knee. "I have to go now. My mother's waiting for this stuff."

"Yeah, me too."

"Are you walking?"

"I've got a bike," I said, waiting for her to leave so she wouldn't see it was a girl's.

"Okay. See ya, Win."

"Yeah, Heather, see ya." I watched her walk off and got things settled in the wire baskets. Heather was nothing like the silly girls I knew in Durango. And all

I did was talk about cooking and never even asked where she lived.

The house was empty and quiet. I put the groceries away and cleaned up Donny's mess. Elliott would never work in a kitchen like that. Next I devised a plan, the way he would: Cook the peas and carrots and douse them in dressing, and while they're soaking make the croques.

Elliott usually had his stereo going while he cooked. I went into Ma's room to borrow her little transistor radio. Her room was a disaster. She had changed clothes at least four times before she settled on what to wear on the picnic and dropped all the rejects on the bed. I turned the dial to find the rock station but on the way picked up something I had heard at Elliott's. Maybe I'd listen for a few minutes to Elliott-type music, since I was cooking an Elliott-type meal, just to get in the mood. I rummaged around for a place mat and a paper napkin. We didn't have any wine glasses. One of these days I'd buy a couple.

While the sandwich fried, I debated what Elliott did when he ate by himself. Did he read a book or just listen to music or what? Did he pour his wine into a special goblet and swirl it around and hold it up to the light and sniff it and taste a little sip if there was nobody there? I laid *Huckleberry Finn* next to my place.

When the sandwich got to looking the way Elliott's did, I flipped it onto a plate and dished up some salad. I poured out the soda and held it up and said, "Salute!" (I didn't learn until later that you're supposed to say "Salud," which means, "Your health." And this was to *my* health.) Meanwhile Ma's radio was cranking out classical music, and I began to think it wasn't such a bad life after all.

The cold carrot and peas were really lukewarm and not as good as Elliott's; he must have done something else to them. But the croque was perfect. I didn't know what Huck and Jim ate when they floated down the Mississippi, but I thought if I ever went on a river trip with Elliott we would surely eat like kings.

I cleaned up the dishes, because that's what Elliott would have done, and took the rest of my soda and went outside to sit on the front step and think about things. I was feeling kind of lonesome. Huck Finn was lonesome a lot too, another thing we had in common. Like the time his pap, which is what he called his terrible father, locked him up in the cabin, and other times when he didn't have anyone to talk to. But there were plenty of times when I felt lonesome even when Donny and Ma and Paul were around and I couldn't talk to any of them about anything important. Donny was just a little kid, and if he missed his pap it wasn't the same pap I missed. Paul was a thoroughly messed-up person, *at least* half a bubble off. Ma was in her own world.

I imagined the kind of conversation I would have if there was somebody to have a conversation with. For instance, if it was Heather, we could talk about whales. Had she ever seen a whale, or did she just read about them? But the only company I had that evening was a visit from Diablo, the black lab come to check out our garbage can.

# SEVENTEEN

## FANTASIES

**T**HIS IS how it was going at the end of July:

Elliott and Paul were still away. Without them the days were all pretty much the same: hot and boring. Ma got Donny and me out of bed every morning when she was ready to leave for work, her hair in a new short style that Hal Norris talked her into. She made sure we were up and had our instructions before she hugged us and left for the day to clean houses. She had a lot of customers now, people who liked the way she took care of their homes sent her to their friends. I always had a few chores, like cleaning up the kitchen or doing the laundry or getting groceries.

After lunch, which was always flufferbanutters because I let Donny fix them, we did things like going to the library. Paul never wanted to stop there when we cruised the Plaza; he preferred the Granny Applesauce scam. But Donny liked it. He'd go down to the kiddy section, and I'd have a hard time dragging him away with fewer than a dozen books.

There was also the possibility that Heather would be at the library. But that isn't where I finally saw her again.

We were at the swimming pool. I didn't like the pool because it was so crowded, all people I didn't know. But Donny pestered me until I gave in. He liked to jump up and down and act silly. He wanted me to come in the water with him, but I said he'd have to find someone else to play with, because I was going to read.

I did what Elliott always did: I took along a book. Elliott said he never went anywhere without a book, in case he had to sit around and wait for an airplane or an appointment or something. I spread out my towel and opened *The Lion, the Witch and The Wardrobe* by C. S. Lewis. Ma found it when she was going through her boxes. She said it was one she liked a lot when she was growing up.

"C. S. Lewis is my favorite writer."

A pair of feet appeared in front of me. Heather's, I discovered. "Is he?" That was all I could think of to say. Dazzling.

"That's part of a whole series set in the magical kingdom of Narnia. I've read them all, a couple of times. Once I even went to a Narnia Camp up in the mountains, to discuss the symbolism and other things. I also like Madeleine L'Engle. Do you know her books?"

"I never heard of her. Actually I don't read much of this kind of thing."

"I do. I like fantasy. Don't you like fantasy?"

"I don't know if I do or not. It was all I could find to bring along. My favorite author is Mark Twain."

"I like him too. Especially *Huckleberry Finn*."

I sat up on my towel, squinting at her with the sun in my eyes. She had on a light blue bathing suit with little white flowers, and she wore a baggy white shirt over it.

"You like *Huck Finn* too?"

"Sure." She laughed. "Makes you want to get a raft, doesn't it? You're going to get sunburned," she said. "Do you have any sunscreen on?"

"No." She was right about that. I burned very easily, and probably in another hour I'd be completely fried.

"I've got some you can use, if you want to."

"You do?"

"I'll be right back."

I had been thinking about Heather Key for days, *weeks*, imagining how when I'd see her again we'd have a lot to say to each other. Now here she was and my mind was blank and my tongue was stuck to the roof of my mouth. One good thing was that Paul was not around to make gross remarks about her big breasts.

Heather came back with the sunscreen and a towel that said "Pittsburgh Steelers" on it. "Listen, is it okay if I sit down?"

"Oh yeah, sure." I moved my old yellow towel with the rust stains on it and made room for her.

She watched me smear lotion on my arms and shoulders and chest, and I felt embarrassed having her look at me like that.

"Make sure you get your nose," she said. "That's the part of me that always burns first."

"Yeah. Thanks." I handed her the bottle. "You come here a lot?"

She began working on her own nose. "Pretty often. I bring my little sister Michelle here. She's out there playing with the kid in the green shorts."

"That's my little brother Donny."

Donny was skinny, all knees and elbows, like me, and Michelle was round, like Heather. It was impossible not to notice that Heather was round. Not fat, just round. Her face was round, too, and pretty, with masses of dark hair and big iris-blue eyes. But I had a hard time not looking at her breasts, spilling out over the top of her bathing suit. I knew that's why she was wearing a big shirt, so not everybody would stare at them. I wondered if everybody believed what Paul did, that girls with big breasts were sex-crazed.

We sat and watched the little kids splash around, and every once in a while, I'd come up with something to say. More often she'd say something, and it got easier. We talked more about fantasy, and I told her I was interested in unicorns. "I have a friend who likes unicorns too. He's kind of an expert on them."

"You mean Elliott M. Deerfield?"

"Yes. How did you know that?"

"It figures he likes unicorns. Tell me about him."

So I told her how hard it was having Elliott for an amigo, because he had all these strange ideas, like photographing wildflowers and going to the opera and cooking. But I didn't tell her the thing about Elliott that worried me. Maybe someday I would.

When it was time to go I called Donny, and Heather collected Michelle, and we gathered up our stuff. Donny put on his thongs and wore his wet suit home, but Michelle insisted on going into the dressing room to shower and change and fix her hair. We left before they came out. I *still* didn't know where Heather lived, but I knew now that she took Michelle to the pool and I'd see her there again. Next time I'd find out her phone number, and maybe I'd call her up sometime and ask her to go for a walk or something.

I whistled the whole way home, and Donny looked at me as if I were at least a half a bubble off.

There was a postcard from Elliott. "Dear Win," he wrote, "A fantastic trip, but I miss Santa Fe, the mountains, the clean air. And you too! Hope all goes well. See you soon. Best, Elliott."

It was a postcard from a museum with a picture of a unicorn lying in a field surrounded by a fence, "The Unicorn in Captivity" that he had told me about.

So far no word from Paul, living the high life in Dallas.

Donny and Ma were going someplace with Hal and Joey. This time they invited me too, but I didn't feel like it. "Thanks anyway," I said, "but I've got some things I want to do this evening."

After I ate—a pasta salad, my latest Elliott-type experiment—I put the postcard in my private drawer and got out the notebook labeled *Spelling and Grammar Exercises*. The notebook was filling up with all kinds of writing. I had started a kind of diary, making notes on my life. And in the back of the notebook I wrote a long letter to Michael X. Kelly in San Diego, explaining why I needed to see him. I wanted to tell him about Elliott and ask his advice, man to man. Ma thought Elliott was terrific, Paul thought he was queer, and I knew that I liked him even if he was unusual. If I liked him and he was gay, did that mean I was gay too? Of course I never mailed the letter.

I tried some stories too, but I never could finish them. I'd go so far, and then I either got tired of it or I didn't know what to do next and quit.

I began a story about a unicorn. The unicorn was very lonely, looking for a mate, but it didn't know that it was the only one in the universe and that it was always destined to be alone. I planned to have it see its reflection in a pool and fall in love with it and jump in after it and drown, and only in death would it find true happiness. But I got depressed with that idea.

The section with true stories Elliott told me went better. I wrote about a boy who ate popcorn for breakfast, instead of cereal, and popcorn for lunch, instead of a sandwich, and popcorn for dinner, pretending it was meat loaf or pork chops. Next I planned to write one about a man who was snowed in in his cabin in the mountains, and the snow was so deep he couldn't get out for two weeks and all he had to eat was canned sardines. And I would write a story about a kid my age who gets caught in quicksand. I would try to describe how he lay there scared and alone watching his backpack disappear and wondering if anybody would find him before he got sucked all the way down or if he would die there, but I hadn't figured out how to rescue my hero in an exciting way.

Sitting by myself on the front step, I decided to write about the life I intended to live some day. I'd have my own place, probably up in the mountains somewhere. It would be a lot like Elliott's house, with shelves full of books and a second floor with a telescope for looking at the stars. I'd build it myself, all of wood, with a fireplace and a kitchen with a butcher block in the middle. I'd hang my own photographs on the walls, and I'd take pictures and write stories and articles and send them off to magazines. I'd write about what it's like to live alone with only a dog and a cat and your own imagination for company.

My dog and I would go out hunting together for rabbits and squirrels, and I'd plant a little garden. I'd learn how to preserve things from my garden and fruit from the trees I'd plant. I'd find berries in the woods. I would bake bread. In winter my dog and my cat and I would settle in with plenty of firewood, and that's when I'd write. I'd get snowshoes and we'd go out and have adventures.

I'd carve a chess set out of wood, and each piece would be different and beautiful. Then I realized I probably wouldn't have anybody to play chess with, and having it would just make me feel more lonesome. I could hear the wind sighing in the pines and an old hoot owl whooing in the distance somewhere.

I'd learn to play the guitar, and I'd make sad music in the evening while the sun went down behind the mountains in the distance. I'd watch the stars come out and have another cup of coffee and maybe a brandy in a crystal glass and listen for the owl.

Maybe I'd save some stranded cross-country skiers who had lost their way, and I'd get them back to my cabin and thaw them out and give them hot chocolate and homemade bread, and they'd recover and be grateful. They'd offer me money as a reward, but of course I wouldn't take it. One of them would be the owner of a big publishing company, and he'd start talking about books, and I'd tell him I was writing one. And he'd say earnestly, "The story of your life would be worth a lot of money to us, Mr. Kelly." And I'd nod and say, "I'll think about it."

We'd sit up talking all night while the others slept, and he'd discover that I was very smart and knew a lot of things. The next morning we'd sit down together at my desk (which I had built and finished myself), and he'd draw up a contract in which he promised to pay me thousands and thousands of dollars for a book called *The Adventures of Win Kelly*. Then I'd cook them all breakfast and we'd talk some more, and the publisher's friend would say that a story like that was really too big for just a book, it should be made into a movie. He'd know people in Hollywood, and he'd see that it was done.

The men would stay with me for a while (sometimes I figured a few days, sometimes several weeks; I knew it was going to be lonely out in that cabin) and I'd show them around the woods and teach them the ways of mountain men. Then, very sadly, they'd say they had to go back to New York City.

I had to work on the next part of the daydream several times to get it right. In one version I led them out on snowshoes; in another I radioed for a helicopter to come and get them. But no matter how I plotted it, the publisher's daughter came to meet him. Sometimes she slid down the rope ladder from the helicopter. Sometimes she came running out of the ski lodge. "Daddy! Daddy! You're safe," she'd holler, and I'd hang back while the two of them hugged and kissed, the way I always thought fathers ought to hug their kids. And then he'd take her by the hand and say, "I want you to meet the young man who saved my life, the brilliant writer Win Kelly." And I'd come forward (to the ski lodge, to the helicopter) and this girl would rush over and hug and kiss me too.

The girl was always Heather Key.

I was still sitting out on the step, lost in my daydream, when Ma and Donny came back with Hal and Joey. The kids tumbled out of the back seat of Hal's new Saab Turbo 900, and Hal hustled around to open the car door for my mother as though she were some fragile princess. Donny and Joey were already headed toward the house, arguing about something as usual. They were like two tomcats, both of them wanting all the attention from Ma and Hal. Hal called to them to get their stuff out of the back seat.

I saw him put his arm around Ma's shoulders. I saw her lean against him and smile up at him. I saw how the two of them looked at each other, and I thought, Here we go again.

Hal had a neat blond mustache and a blow-dried haircut. He wore a school ring with a big blue stone. He was lean and tanned, from playing a lot of tennis, and he worked out at Nautilus. Elliott scorned Nautilus as being another American peculiarity, that you have to go some special place to get exercise, but Hal went there every day, and he tried to get Ma to join too. Hal also played golf, which Elliott considered a ridiculous activity. "Golf isn't a sport," Elliott once

said. "It's a game, like bowling." I had begun to understand that Elliott was a terrible snob.

"Hal's in real estate," Ma told me the next day
when she came home from work. "He says he can get
me a good job in his company when I finish my word-
processing course, and he says that would be the first
step toward a much better job, depending on what my
career goals are."

Career goals? I never heard Ma talk that way
before.

"What are your career goals?"

She shrugged. "To make money. Hal says the way
to get started in his company is in some sort of secre-
tarial job, and they'll see how talented I am, and I can
go on from there. Maybe even end up as a real estate
broker."

"Elliott thinks you should be an artist."

"He does?"

"Remember those sketches? He's got them
framed and hanging in his office. And Dr. Vogel keeps
talking about your unicorn jackets."

"Wow," she said, and sat down on her bed to
think that one over. Then the phone rang, and she
jumped up and raced for it. "That might be Hal."

I tried to imagine Heather racing for the phone if
I called her up. I couldn't. She was the kind of girl
who'd be right at home in a cabin in the mountains.

# EIGHTEEN

—•—

## STAR-SPANGLED COOKIES

**H**EATHER was definitely not the kind of girl who raced for the phone.

I was in the kitchen mixing bread dough when I heard somebody at the door. Donny hurtled into the kitchen yelling, "That girl is here!"

"What girl?" I wiped my hands on my pants and went to see who he was talking about. It was Heather.

I instantly got totally self-conscious. I had been dumping flour into the bowl while some canned ravioli heated in the pan for Donny, who stuck up his nose at my gourmet experiments. I was actually thinking about Heather and the kinds of things we could talk about when I saw her the next time. But when she sort of materialized out of my imagination I acted like an idiot without a thought in my head.

"You didn't come to the pool yesterday or today,"

she said, "so I thought I'd bring you the book we talked about." It was *A Wrinkle in Time by* Madeleine L'Engle.

"How did you know where I live?" asked this not-too-bright person who seemed to be inhabiting my brain temporarily.

"I was here at your yard sale, remember? That's where I met you."

"Oh yeah. Right." Desperate pause.

"Are you busy? Donny said you were cooking supper."

"I think I'm *burning* supper. Come on!"

She followed me to the kitchen, where flour was scattered everywhere and the canned ravioli was definitely scorched. I grabbed the pan off the stove and cursed it, but not so that it would offend Heather.

"You really *do* know how to make bread."

"Do it all the time," I bragged untruthfully. "I'm getting to be a pretty good cook. Elliott's teaching me how."

"What else can you make?"

"Well, there's croque monsieur, of course, and pasta sauce," and I talked on and on because I was afraid to stop once I got started. "I'll cook a whole meal for you some time, start to finish. You'll see."

Her eyebrows arched.

"You don't believe me?"

She smiled, the kind of white-toothed smile you saw in ads with kids who never got cavities. "I believe you. But you really ought to prove it."

"I will. I'll cook you a meal you'll never forget!"

"Are you intending to eat that stuff?" she asked, peering at the ravioli.

"I'm not hungry," I said. The ravioli was hot, only a little scorched, and Donny would be out any second in search of food. "Do you want to go for a walk after I give this to Donny? I have to babysit, but I can be gone for a little while."

This was a historical moment in the life of Win Kelly: I was always hungry, and before that instant I did not believe that I would rather be with a girl than eat. I scraped all the ravioli in a bowl, got a big spoon, and took it to Donny, who was, of course, on the floor in front of the TV.

"I'm going out for a little while, okay?" I said. "Just to the store for a soda."

He nodded, already stuffing in the ravioli. "Bring me something," he said, and I figured I could get him some M&Ms and everything would be fine.

I grabbed a couple of dollars out of my secret hiding place in *Spelling and Grammar*. Heather and I walked toward the Circle K. A car full of guys cruised by and one of them started yelling out the window at Heather. I recognized Paul's buddy Ross from the yard sale.

Heather turned away and crammed her hands in the pockets of a jacket she wore even though it was really hot. I felt like punching the guy, but they had driven off and even if he hadn't I wasn't any kind of fighter. I felt embarrassed and miserable.

"I don't understand what it is about guys and girls' breasts," she said, staring at where her sneakers were going. "They gawk at them because they're big, and they all seem to think if you have big breasts you're doing sex all the time. Even a lot of girls think that."

She quit studying her sneakers and looked straight at me. "Do *you* understand it?"

I shook my head. This was a very difficult conversation.

"I thought maybe you could explain it, you being a boy and all."

"I can't. I mean, I don't really know why guys think that. Maybe it's because guys don't really know much about girls, so they make up a lot of stupid stuff. It's almost as though girls were a whole different kind of human. I can't begin to imagine what it's like to be a girl."

"I can't imagine what it's like to be a boy. Do you think because our bodies are so different, our heads are different too?"

"Probably. I've seen pictures in, uhh, in men's magazines, and I don't know, it seems very mysterious."

"The girls in those pictures all have big breasts, right?"

"Well, yeah, I guess so."

"Which makes them automatically sexy. I wonder if their big breasts give them as much trouble as mine do."

"Trouble?" I said, kind of stupidly, but this conversation was completely out of control, and I didn't know what to say that wasn't stupid.

"Backaches, for one thing. And for another the way guys leer at you and girls tell each other you're a tramp. But all that's about to change for me. I'm having an operation."

"Operation?" When you're as lost as I was, all you can do is repeat the last word someone has said.

"I'm going in the hospital in two weeks for surgery to have them made smaller."

I didn't know such a thing was possible. I was relieved when we got to the Circle K and I could think of something else. I had enough money for a couple of cans of soda and some M&Ms to buy off Donny, but Heather pulled out her wallet and said, "I'm a liberated woman. I pay my own way."

We looked for a place to sit and drink them, but the traffic was roaring by and the air was gray with exhaust fumes. I got the bright idea of going to the blockhouse, which wasn't far away. It would be quiet there, at least.

"Smells bad but it's a good hideout," she said, peering around inside. "What do you do here?"

"This is where Paul and I come to talk when we have to get away from home," I explained. "Paul's an army freak. Did you know that? Do you know him from school?"

She shook her head. "I've just seen him around with his obscene friends."

"Anyway, he's in uniform most of the time, and we come here for what he calls 'debriefings.'"

"About what?" She sat down on a concrete block, and so did I.

"Lately it's mostly about Elliott Deerfield."

"What about Elliott?"

She had told me this thing about her breasts, and now I thought maybe Heather Key was the person to talk to about Elliott and the thing that worried me most. So I took a real deep breath and said, "Paul thinks Elliott is, uh, sort of different."

"I'd say he's a whole lot different. I'd say he's probably pretty unusual even in a place like Santa Fe. This town is a refuge for unusual people, you know."

"Unusual how?"

"Oh, artists, writers, hippies, dropouts, people getting over broken hearts, people going through a midlife crisis. That's why we came here. My father was having a midlife crisis."

"What do you mean by that?"

"He was working for a big corporation in Pittsburgh, and he decided he didn't want that any more, so we moved out here and they opened that cookie shop on the Plaza. You know Star-Spangled Cookies?"

"Yeah, I know where it is." The cookies cost about seventy-five cents apiece.

"They named it that because of our great-great-great-great-great-great-grandfather, Francis Scott Key, who wrote 'The Star-Spangled Banner.' All the cookies are stars and flags and eagles and so on."

"That's your parents?"

"Yes, they're real characters. So why did Elliott come here? I bet he's not a native Santa Fean."

"I don't know exactly why. He used to live in Houston, I think, but he's originally from Baltimore, Maryland."

"Probably came here to find himself."

"Find himself what?"

She laughed, even though it was a stupid joke. "Is he married? A lot of men come here to get over their divorces. Women too."

"Elliott's never been married."

"No?" She was silent for a minute, draining off the last drops of her soda. "Oh, I get it! You think he's gay!"

"I don't think so," I said, dropping little bits of grass and dirt through the hole of my empty can.

"But the Little General does."

"Little General?"

"Paul."

"Yeah, I guess so." I mashed the can flat.

"So what do you care what Paul thinks?"

"How can I *not* care what he thinks? He's my best friend."

"Hooee, you need new friends, that's all I can say. First of all, I think he's wrong. Second, even if he's right, so what?"

"Paul says the kids at school will find out I have a gay amigo and they'll think I'm gay too."

"And you care about that?"

"Hey, what's making you so brave all of a sudden? You're the one who's upset because everybody thinks you're a tramp because your tits are so big!"

We both got real quiet, real quick, because I should never have said anything like that to anybody, and certainly not to Heather who was trying to help. But there was a little bit of truth in it and she knew it. That's what made her quiet too. I guess we both felt bad.

"Hey, Heather, I'm sorry I said that."

"Yeah, well, Win, I guess you're right. I should know what it's like to have people making wrong judgments about you."

I got up and stood in the doorway. "When are you going to the hospital?" I asked her.

"Week from Monday."

"You scared?"

"It's no big deal."

"Who says?"

"The plastic surgeon. And my mom. So I guess it's not."

"But they put you to sleep and everything, right?"

"Yes."

"And it hurts when you wake up, right?"

"Some."

"So that makes it a big deal."

I had to get home because of Donny. He was alone in the house and who knows what kind of trouble he could get into. We hurried back, not talking much.

"You can have the rest of Elliott's magazines if you want them. Take some now and I'll bring the rest to your house sometime."

"Thanks. That's really nice of you."

I tossed Donny his M&Ms and brought out a small armful of *Scientific Americans* so I'd have an excuse to make a couple of trips myself.

"Will you be at the pool tomorrow?"

"Yes. Will you?"

"Yes."

We grinned at each other like two simple fools. When she was gone I got my notebook. I had a lot to write down.

# NINETEEN

## MIDLIFE CRISIS

**E**LLIOTT'S VOICE sounded hollow on the telephone, long distance. "How's everything in Santa Fe?" he asked.

"Great," I said. "Where are you? I thought you'd be home by now."

"I thought so too. That's why I'm calling. I'm in Boston. I came up here yesterday, and it looks as though I'm going to be here for several days. Then I have to fly to Los Angeles and on down to San Diego. It's going to be another ten days to two weeks until I get home. Some of our plans will have to go on hold."

"That's okay." Okay because I had plenty of things to do with Heather, and I wasn't exactly going crazy missing him but I didn't tell him that.

"What have you been doing?"

"Reading," I said. "And swimming. I take Donny

to the pool almost every day." That made me sound like a terrific person, watching out for my little brother, but of course the reason I did it was to see Heather. We sat and talked while the little kids played in the pool.

"Good! What are you reading?"

"I finished *Huck Finn* and now I'm reading the Narnia books by C. S. Lewis, and a book by Madeleine L'Engle." I figured Elliott wouldn't know about writers of kids' books, but that just shows I would always misjudge Elliott.

"Excellent! C. S. Lewis is one of the great religious writers of our time," Elliott said, lecturing all the way from Boston on long-distance rates. "And you may not believe this one, but Madeleine L'Engle is an old friend of mine. She's a wonderful woman, an absolutely brilliant writer. I once even thought I was in love with her, before she married Hugh."

Elliott in love? Was this the proof I needed for Paul? When Elliott came back, I would get him to tell me stories about his early romance, and then I would report it all to Paul.

I hadn't heard a word from Paul since he left for Dallas.

"Guess what, Elliott," I said. "I've baked bread and made spaghetti with tuna fish and about six croques. When you come back, I'm going to make you a real gourmet meal."

"Why, that's quite impressive, Win! I'm proud of you!"

I knew he was. "Did you say you're going to San Diego?"

"Yes, I'll be there about four days and fly home from there."

"That's where my father lives," I said.

"Yes, I remember your telling me that."

"His name is Michael X. Kelly. He lives on Atlantic Drive, or he used to." I struggled with the next part. "Could you find out if he's still there?"

"You can do that yourself, Win. Just call up the information operator and ask for his number."

"I never thought of that."

"That's what I'd do, if I were you."

"Yeah."

"It's not appropriate for me to make the contact. It's up to you."

"Right."

He changed the subject. "When I come back we'll go camping up by Puye Cliffs. I think you'd enjoy that."

"Sounds good."

"I'll be back two weeks from Saturday, at the latest. I'll need a couple of days to get organized, and then we'll go. Mark it on your calendar."

"Great." I tried to sound enthusiastic, but I was still thinking about my father.

"I've got to run now. See you in two weeks."

I looked up the area code for San Diego and called for the number of Michael X. Kelly on Atlantic Drive. The operator said, "I'm sorry, I don't have anyone by that name. There are several Michael Kellys, but none on Atlantic. And no Michael X."

"Thank you."

So much for that. Unless he moved and dropped the X.

*  *  *

"Elliott's not coming back for two more weeks," I told Heather.

We were at our usual spot at the pool, where we met almost every day. While the little kids screamed and thrashed in the water, Heather and I sat like two old people and talked. Heather reminded me to put on sunscreen, and thanks to her I did not fry.

In spite of what I told her, that she did not look ridiculous, Heather refused to take off the big shirt she wore over her bathing suit. She was counting the days until she would go to the hospital for the operation to make her breasts smaller; she was both scared and anxious to get it over with. I didn't blame her. I wouldn't want to go through anything like that, but I wouldn't want people staring and making nasty remarks either.

We didn't talk about it. I took it as a challenge to keep her mind off it.

In the evenings when I had to stay with Donny, Heather came to my house and we sat outside on the step. When Donny and Ma went somewhere with Hal and Joey, I walked over to her place, and we sat out on the patio.

Her parents seemed to like having me around. Her father, Scott Key, was a quiet, serious person, but her mother, Frances, never seemed to shut up. ("Yes, her name really *is* Frances. They've spent sixteen years of married life explaining it.") Heather looked like her mother, but she had her own personality, sometimes bubbly, other times serious.

They had bought an old adobe in our part of town, the *barrio*, which was an unusual thing for Anglos to do, and they were slowly fixing it up. Mr. Key did all the work on it, when he wasn't up at the Star Spangled Cookie. He had remodeled the bathrooms, built a solar greenhouse, and he was laying bricks for a patio. Every time I went over, part of the house was torn up.

Mrs. Key ran the cookie store, which was now shipping sugar cookies in patriotic tin boxes all over the country and even to an exclusive department store in Dallas, and she was also involved in several clubs and political organizations. They had been in Santa Fe about a year, and already Mrs. Key had formed a citizens' group to halt the building of a huge new bank that she insisted would ruin the character of the Plaza.

"It was exactly like this in Pittsburgh," Heather said. "My dad spent all his spare time remodeling our house, and my mom ran organizations. They never just *relaxed*."

"My mother's out all the time too." I had already explained about her jobs and school. "Even when she's home, I'm not sure she's really *there*, if you know what I mean."

"I do. Midlife crisis or not, nothing has really changed. They still run at top speed. My dad may seem quiet, but he is intense. Very intense! My mom does all the talking, but my dad is really the one who goes for it. Like the cookie store. That was his idea, and he set it all up, even though Mom runs it. Has your mother had a midlife crisis?"

"All the time," I said. "I never know what's happening next. I'm not sure what a midlife crisis is, but she's had three husbands and I think she's falling in love again, and if it isn't a crisis for her it sure is for me."

"Who's she in love with this time?"

"His name is Hal, and he's Donny's amigo."

Hal had started meeting Ma at the restaurant where she played guitar and bringing her home after work. A few nights before I woke up and thought she was just coming home; it was getting light outside. Then I realized it wasn't Ma coming, it was Hal going. She had said never again, and I hoped she meant it, because she was so miserable when it broke up. I didn't remember what she was like when my own father left, but it was a disaster after Bobby Don Willett and Joe Favello, and I didn't want to see her that bad again. Maybe it would be different this time with Hal. I sure hoped so. Heather had both parents and I wasn't sure she'd understand how I felt, so I didn't tell her any more.

Heather probably saw me get quiet and thoughtful, because she changed the subject. "Win Kelly," she said, "you once promised to cook me a gourmet dinner. You made a lot of noise about what a fantastic chef you are. When do you intend to prove it?"

"Thursday," I said. "Three days should give you time to fast."

Heather laughed. "That reminds me—want some cookie crumbles?"

She had a sack of broken stars in her swim bag, and we munched through them.

"Wonder when Paul's coming back," I said. "I know you don't care much, but I'm curious about how his trip was to Dallas."

She looked at me oddly. "He's back," she said.

"He is? How do you know?"

"I saw him in the Circle K."

"When was that?"

"About a week ago."

A week ago? Paul had been back that long and hadn't called me? Something wild must have happened in Dallas.

# TWENTY

## CROWSER'S REPORT

**R**EPORT to the block-house for a debriefing," I ordered.

I figured he'd either play along or wipe me out for exceeding authority, but all he said was, "Maybe tomorrow."

I waited another day, then one more, and by then I knew there was trouble of some kind.

Something had happened, that was plain. He wouldn't look me in the eye. Instead he wandered around the blockhouse, squinting at the walls, kicking the floor with the toe of his sneaker. "You been coming here a lot, Kelly?"

"Once," I said, not telling him that it had been with Heather. "Why?"

"Things have changed."

"Changed? How?"

"I don't know. It just feels different." he moved slowly, studying the rough walls, the dirt floor. "Don't you feel it?"

"I don't feel anything different."

He scowled. "You wouldn't."

I was getting annoyed. "So what is it, then?"

"Bad vibes," he said, still pacing and examining things. "Somebody's been here, that's for sure."

"I guess whoever they are they have as much right to be here as we do. Ma always said she thought drug dealers or derelicts use this place at night and we shouldn't come here."

"And you always do what Mommy says."

I had no idea what was eating this creep, but it was time to change the subject before I wasted him. "How was the trip?" I finally asked.

He shrugged and jammed his fists in the pockets of his fatigues. "Okay, I guess."

"Did your dad meet you at the airport in a Mercedes?"

"Yeah."

"What model?" I kept after him.

"A 450 SL. Yellow with black leather seats. He calls it 'The Lemon.' That's the name he gave it— you know, because of the color, not because it isn't a great car."

"I get it," I said. "Does he live in a nice place?"

"Yeah, it's okay. It's an apartment complex called Tudor Towers, and the buildings all have fake fronts that make them look like Old English houses. Inside it's not Old English at all. It's got white shag carpet and a wet bar and a balcony overlooking the swimming pool, and there's an exercise room downstairs and a sauna."

"Did you just hang around there or what?"

"We went places. Out to eat and so on."

Which didn't sound bad to me, so what was eating him? Then I had an idea: "Is your Dad remarried?"

His head came up and he looked at me and laughed, a bitter sound. "No. No, he's not married. He's got a lover, though."

I knew how uncomfortable that could be, because before Ma married Joe Favello he hung around all the time, and he'd leave before we got up in the morning but I knew that he was there and it didn't fool me, if that was their intention. Now the same thing was happening with Hal. I guessed it was just as bad when a father had a girl friend.

So I said sympathetically, "That can be a bummer. I suppose she was hanging around all the time, being nice to you, and you know the main reason she's doing it is not because she's so crazy about you but because she's trying to make a good impression on your father. Playing family and all that craperoo." Ma had said there weren't going to be any more men after Joe Favello, and she hadn't kept her word. "You'd think she'd be able to cool it for a week, at least, so you and your dad could spend some time alone."

"If only it was a girl friend!" Paul said, mumbling so I could hardly understand him.

"What?"

"My father's lover is a *guy*. My father is a freaking faggot!" He leaned against the rough wall and started to cry.

I felt so bad for him I didn't know what to do, and so I sat down on a concrete block and peeled off some sunburned skin and listened to him sob. After a while he wiped his nose on his sleeve. "You ever tell anybody and I'll beat the crap out of you." He tried to say it in his army voice, but he was shaking and didn't sound tough at all.

"I won't. Did he come right out and tell you, or did you figure it out for yourself?"

"It was like this. The first day we went and rode around and he showed me the sights, where President Kennedy was assassinated and so on. We picked up Chinese food and ate out by the pool, and he introduced me to some of the neighbors. I thought some of them seemed pretty faggish. The next day was more of the same, the zoo and the botanical gardens. He told me a friend of his was coming for dinner.

"This guy, Davey, arrives, and he's got a sack of groceries. The two of them go into the kitchen, which you can see from the living room, and start cooking. I notice that Davey knows where everything belongs, like he spends a lot of time there. In fact it almost seems like it's his home. But I'm watching television and not paying that much attention. We eat and the guy leaves and Dad asks me what I think of Davey, and I tell him he seems okay to me. And Dad says he hopes I like him, because that's his best friend in the whole world.

"The next night Davey is back again, and we all go out to the movies and for ice cream afterwards. The day after that Davey takes off from work and the three of us drive to Six Flags, which is sort of Texas Disneyland. By then I'm getting sick of Davey, even though he's nice and all. Davey leaves early that evening and Dad says, 'Pauly'—that's what he called me when I was little, Pauly—'I want to talk to you. This is a very hard thing for me to say.'

"I don't say nothing, and then he comes out with it: 'Pauly, I'm a homosexual. Davey is my lover. It's a committed relationship.'

"I start to yell and carry on, because I'm so upset I don't know what to do. 'I hope you get AIDS,' I scream at him. You know—that terrible disease that fags get that kills them. Mom says it's God's vengeance against perverted sex. 'And don't ever call me Pauly again,' I holler.

"Dad cries, and I cry, and he says he knows how hard it is to hear something like this, but he wants to explain, he wants me to understand, because even though his 'sexual orientation' is different he is still my father and he still loves me.

"I ask him has he always been gay, and he says he supposes so but he didn't really admit it to himself until a few years ago, and that's when he and my mom got a divorce. He says he hated himself for a long time, but now that he's met Davey he's settled down. He says I really have Davey to thank for him getting in touch with me.

"The next day when he went to the basement to check the laundry, I snooped around and found a picture of him and Davey, hugging each other. The picture is in a frame, and I figured that picture of them hugging was probably on top of his desk until I came, and Davey probably lives there and sleeps in the big bed and moved out temporarily while I was there.

"You know what he wants me to do? He wants

me to come to Dallas and live with him and Davey. He
says we'd get a bigger place, maybe in the same apartment complex, and I'd have my own room. He says
when I get used to the idea I'll see that it isn't any
worse and maybe a whole lot better than living with
my mom. He says living with him won't make me gay.
'It's not contagious,' he says. He claims Mom is so
screwed up she could do me a lot more damage than he
ever could."

Finally Paul quit talking. I didn't know what to
say or to think.

"Did you ever tell your mom all this?"

"Not that part. I said I found out he's gay. I don't
want to talk to her about it."

"Jeez, Paul! What do you want to do?"

"Run away. I don't want nothing to do with either
one of them. I just want to get out of here. And there's
no place to go."

Paul started to cry again. I wanted to put my hand
on his shoulder and tell him I understood how bad he
felt. But there was no way in the world I was going to
touch him now.

I confess that the first thing I did when I got home
was to get out *Spelling and Grammar Exercises* and
write down everything Paul told me about his father
and Davey, everything I could remember.

The second thing I did was to call Heather.

# TWENTY-ONE

## THE BLOCKHOUSE

THE KELLY-KEY Diners Club, named by Heather, was planning its first major event. Heather said if I'd cook one fantastic meal for her, she'd cook one fantastic meal for me the next time.

"You'll be taking a severe risk, though," she said. "You have Elliott to teach you, and I have nobody."

"Doesn't your mother cook?"

"Not very often. She's too busy at the shop to bother, so she gets take-out food from one of those elegant shops near the store. We eat beautiful food but I'm never sure what it is. And I'm certainly not learning how to cook it. Not even cookies."

"Do they know about Edible Collages?" I described PizzArt constructions of anchovies and capers and other foreign bodies.

"I can't get over you," Heather said. "You've been here two months, and you know a lot more about this town than I do."

"Thanks to Elliott."

"I know. Is he back yet?"

"In a few more days."

"I'll bet you'll be glad to see him."

"Yeah." That was true, but it was also true that it didn't matter as much now as it did before I met her.

"How's the Little General? Did you finally get to see him?"

"Yesterday at the blockhouse."

"How was his trip to Dallas? He get along all right with his father?"

I had been arguing with myself since the day before about what I would say to Heather. I promised Paul I wouldn't tell anybody, but I made an exception for her. For one thing, she wasn't the kind of person who went blabbing everything. If the story of Paul's father got around, it wouldn't be because of Heather.

Second, I figured he owed her one, for all the ugly things he had said about her and her breasts. Now she'd know something that made him feel bad, and that evened the score.

Third, Heather was my best friend, a lot closer than Paul now, and I felt I *ought* to share it with her, even though that meant breaking my word to Paul, who had been my friend for much longer.

So I unreeled the whole story, the way Paul had told it to me, and the way I had recorded it in *Spelling and Grammar*.

"That's harsh," she said. In fact that's all she said. I thought maybe she'd get a sense of justice done for the miserable things he had said about her, but if that's how she felt, she didn't say it. Just: "That's harsh."

I shifted gears. "Hal says the property with the blockhouse has been sold to a developer. They're going to build condos on it."

"You'll have to find a new hideout," she said. Did she mean for Paul and me or for her and me? Either way, she was right. I'd miss the ratty old dump.

"Paul was real uneasy when we were there yesterday. He was sure somebody had been using it. Ma never did want us going there. She's been convinced all along that druggies and other characters hang out at the blockhouse at night."

"My mother is like that too. She sees danger lurking behind every tree, and I tell her she has to learn to trust life. You can't go around thinking there's always somebody ready to attack you."

"Elliott says he's more afraid of weak people than he is of muggers and thieves and murderers. Did I ever tell you the story about Elliott getting stuck in quicksand?"

"Yes," she said, "you did."

I guess I had told her most of my Elliott stories.

"We should go to the blockhouse one last time before they tear it down," I said.

"Good," she said. "Why don't we go there for the ultimate gourmet dining experience?"

"*What* ultimate gourmet dining experience?"

"The one you promised to create. You *are* going to keep your word, aren't you?"

"Of course I'm going to keep my word," I huffed. "Even though it's much harder to keep my word in the blockhouse than it is in our kitchen."

"Never thought you'd shrink from a challenge, Win Kelly."

*Menu*: pasta salad with tuna fish and peas and walnuts (learned from Elliott, naturally) two slices of my own homemade bread, and fresh raspberries with yogurt and brown sugar sauce.

I packed it all in a bucket, the way Paul did, and threw in some napkins and a couple of candle stubs and an old pillowcase for a tablecloth. This would be a good luck party for Heather, who was getting nervous about her surgery and pretending not to be.

Heather brought two wine glasses from home and an insulated cooler with four cans of soda. I set the table and arranged the food, and the Kelly–Key Diners Club sat down to eat.

I held my glass up and swirled and sniffed and tasted the Dr Pepper. The pasta salad and bread turned out to be pretty good but not as good as croques, and the raspberries were first class. The candles were burning, and it was pretty but not very comfortable. I took the cloth off the makeshift table and spread it on the ground for Heather, so we could lean against the wall and Heather wouldn't get her white shorts dirty.

"Do you realize we'll be sitting near each other in some of our classes?" I asked.

"Only where teachers are into alphabetical order," she said. "Mostly here they are. In Pittsburgh I had one teacher who seated people chronologically, just to be different—got everybody's birthdate and had them sit according to the order in which they were born. Her name was Miss Snodgrass, and she did little astrological charts for each of us. Every class period she'd call attention to anything special that might be going on for the Libras or the Leos or whoever."

"What class was that?"

"Oh, Snoddy taught a sort of social studies class, but it was a lot more than that. I miss her."

"School starts in three weeks," I said. I wasn't looking forward to that. It was always hard to figure everything out in a new school that everybody else already knew.

One can of soda was left. We divided it between the two wine glasses and drank a toast.

"To the new student body," Heather said, clinking glasses.

"Yeah. To the first year of senior high."

"That's not what I meant. It's a joke, Win!"

"Joke? I don't get it."

"The 'new student body' I'm referring to is *mine*."

Oh. Surgery was only four days away.

I never heard them coming, and neither did Heather. Suddenly four guys were crowding in the narrow doorway, staring at us sitting on the dirt floor in the candlelight.

They were eighteen or nineteen years old, in jeans with wide leather belts and sleeveless shirts, their dark hair worn kind of long. We started to get up, but one of them, a porky guy with a headband and a missing front tooth, pushed me back down with his foot. He wore heavy boots.

They let Heather scramble to her feet. She began to explain in a high tense voice that we were just having a picnic and we'd get our stuff togther and clear out right away. "My folks are expecting me any minute," she said. "They know where I am and they'll be over here looking for me."

I thought that was smart. But they didn't believe her. Or they were too drunk to care.

A guy with a scraggly little beard grabbed her and ripped off her big shirt; she had on a regular tee shirt under it. The bearded one pointed to her breasts and laughed. He turned to the others and said something I didn't understand.

One of them reached for her, and I came up off the floor yelling. The guy with the headband pinned my arms, another crooked an elbow across my throat and cut off my air every time I struggled or tried to yell. The other two grabbed Heather.

They shoved her to the ground. I tried one more time to yell, but the arm tightened hard across my windpipe. I didn't quite pass out, but I wished I had when I saw what they were doing to her.

When they were done they dropped me and left. I threw up, and threw up again, and dragged myself over to where Heather lay.

"Are you okay?" I croaked. Stupid question; what I meant was, "Are you still alive?" She rolled her head slowly from side to side. No crying, no nothing. I ripped open the pillow case and wrapped it around her torn shorts and helped her stand up. We were both shaking so hard we could hardly walk. We staggered to my house. Nobody was home. Heather lay curled on the floor while I called the police. Then I called her parents. They all arrived about the same time. I was in a daze. I don't remember much, except that her mother got hysterical and started screaming.

Questions, questions. I couldn't answer them except to keep repeating, I don't know, I don't know. Maybe the police were figuring I had something to do with it. They took Heather away to the hospital, probably the same hospital where she was going to have her surgery. I wondered in a fuzzy way if she could have it done while she was there.

They took me to police headquarters and had me look at mug shots and made me tell the story over and over, explain what we were doing there, how I knew about the place. They made me take them there; I showed them where it was, but I didn't want to go inside. The cops came out with the wine glasses and the bucket and asked what we had been drinking. I told them Dr Pepper and diet soda, but they took the glasses to the lab to test.

I had left a note at home for Ma, and she was at police headquarters when they brought me back from the blockhouse. The cops didn't seem to notice that I wasn't looking too good, but Ma did and got real upset. I was glad Hal was with her. After a while the police let them take me home. Ma hung onto me, crying, and I hung onto her.

"I told you never to go there at night, Win!" she said. I knew she had been right and it was my fault that it had happened. I also knew Heather might blame me, and for sure her parents would.

I asked Ma over and over if she thought Heather would be okay.

"Never completely," Ma said. "She'll never completely forget."

# TWENTY-TWO

## EVERYTHING BEAUTIFUL

**M**RS. KEY wouldn't let me talk to Heather. Every day I called and asked how she was and got a short, cold answer: "The same." And when I asked if I could speak to her, the answer was, "She can't talk to you."

Did that mean she wasn't able to talk to me or didn't want to talk to me or that her mother wouldn't let her? I didn't know.

I wanted to take something to her, a present that would show her how much I cared about her, that I was thinking of her. Then I remembered the broken glass of Irish crystal in my drawer, still wrapped in paper napkins. I had to laugh as I got them out. I did the same thing Ma did—saved odds and ends that used to be beautiful, thinking I'd fix them, make them beautiful again, and then never getting around to it.

But this time I was going to do it. At least I'd be doing something.

I bought a tube of special cement, laid out the three pieces, and began to work carefully. Donny came in while I was stroking on the cement with a toothpick and got his nose within a couple of inches of it.

"Keep away or I'll put crazy glue on your nose."

"Is that crazy glue? Ma says you're not supposed to use that stuff. She says it's dangerous."

"It's some other kind of glue. But if you don't back off you're still going to get glue on your nose."

"What is that?"

"It's a little glass made of Irish crystal."

"Where did you get it?"

"Elliott gave it to me."

"How come Elliott gave you a broken glass?"

And so on and so forth. I set it aside to dry. You could tell it had been broken and stuck back together if you looked at it carefully, but it was still beautiful.

When I was sure it was dry, I wrapped the glass in tissue paper, put on clean jeans and my most decent tee shirt, and went over to Heather's house. Maybe if I actually showed up, her mother would let me speak to her. Maybe Heather would hear my voice and come out to see me.

Mrs. Key looked very tired when she came to the door. She had even lost some weight, or else she was wearing baggy clothes. "Could I please see Heather for just a few minutes?" I said as politely as I knew how. "I have something to give her." I showed her the little package.

"I'm not going to let you see Heather," she said. "Not today, not ever. It's nothing against you, Win.

It's just that you're a reminder of something horrible that happened."

"But I'm her friend," I pleaded. I struggled to keep tears from creeping into my eyes.

"Heather has been through hell," she said, folding her arms across her chest. "I don't think you can possibly understand that."

"I can understand some," I said. "I was there, and I saw it, and I saw the hell she was going through. I wish I hadn't."

"What happened in that wretched shack you took her to, for reasons I cannot begin to comprehend, was just the beginning. There it was her body that went through hell. Now she goes through it with her mind." Mrs. Key began wrenching dead blossoms off the geraniums around the portal with a fierceness the poor flowers did not deserve. "You can't possibly understand," she said. "You're a male. Heather tells me you're a nice boy, but you're still a male, and underneath you're all alike. Animals! It would not surprise me at all to hear that you got some vicarious pleasure out of watching it."

I didn't know what vicarous meant, until I went home and looked up the word in Ma's dictionary, but I knew there had been no pleasure in it. Every time I thought about it my stomach turned over, and I knew that I would never *not ever* forget what I saw in the blockhouse that night.

I wondered if Mrs. Key talked like that to Mr. Key, about all males being animals. I put the package away in my drawer until I found some other way to get the Irish glass to Heather.

* * *

"There's nothing you can do about it," Ma said. "You'll just have to leave it alone, let it go and let whatever is going to happen, happen."

She may have been talking to herself then too. The next week Hal and Joey flew to Minneapolis, where Hal was going to visit his parents for a family reunion before Joey went back to his mother's. I could tell that Ma missed him, but I didn't care: I was glad to have Ma around again.

I stopped calling, and I gave up trying to get past Heather's mother, who guarded her like a dragon. I packed the Irish glass in cotton and mailed it with a note: "Everything beautiful can be mended. Your friend, Win."

A week later I saw her at the library.

"I'm sorry I haven't called you back," she said in a whisper.

"It's okay," I lied.

"It seems to be taking me a long time to feel all right again," she said. "I had to go back to the psychiatrist, the same one who recommended the surgery, and talk and talk about it, to 'work it through,' he keeps saying. And everything is going crazy at home. Mom made my dad move out, because she says he's a male and an oppressor. Then things started to crumble at Star Spangled Cookies"—she smiled a little when she saw I got her joke—"and they've decided to sell the business. We're moving to San Francisco where nobody knows what's happened, and my parents are going to get some counselling."

"They think it was my fault, don't they?"

She wouldn't look at me. "I guess they do."

"Do you?"

No answer.

"Heather, please look at me and answer me. Do you think it was my fault?"

She sighed. "I wish you had been able to help me."

"Oh God, Heather, so do I! So do I! But there were four of them. I couldn't do anything at all!"

"My head knows that. I could see them choking you every time you tried to move or yell. But my stomach says . . . that you could have done something. I know that doesn't make sense."

"No, it doesn't. Heather, I thought you knew all along that I wasn't like the other guys. I never made fun of your breasts. I thought we were good friends. I thought it was special for us."

"It was. You were. We were. But when something like this happens, nothing is enough." She reached over and took my hand, and I rubbed my thumb over her fingers. "I'll write to you from San Francisco. Thanks for the pretty glass. It probably has a story behind it, but I have to go now. My mom's waiting for me. You can keep A Wrinkle in Time," she whispered.

I watched her go and put my head down on the library table so nobody could see I was crying.

# TWENTY-THREE

—•—

# ELLIOTT'S PLANS

**T**HIS WAS the lonesomest I'd ever been. Paul kept to himself, Donny had an amigo, Ma was in love, I couldn't see Heather. Everything had gone wrong. There was not a single thing to feel good about.

So I stuck my face in a book and kept it there. I read the Narnia books by C. S. Lewis. Ma found me *The Catcher in the Rye* at a garage sale. I read *A Wrinkle in Time*, which Heather gave me, and then I read it again.

I wrote in *Spelling and Grammar* every day. I could not write about what had happened to Heather, but I did describe how pretty she was, how smart and funny, how good I felt when we were together. I had wanted to show off for her—cook fancy food, impress her with what a great chef I was, what a gourmet. I sure impressed her, all right. I couldn't protect her, couldn't take care of her, let that terrible thing happen to her. The picture of her beautiful iris-colored eyes, huge and blank with terror, stayed in my mind. I woke up at night yelling for help, but I could never change what happened, even in my dream.

Elliott came back from his trip during that black, painful time. Our six-weeks trial period was up, and we celebrated by going out for enchiladas. We shook hands and agreed to be amigos for another year. I was still scared of all kinds of things about Elliott, including losing him too for whatever reason. I was MISERY spelled in capital letters.

If he noticed anything was wrong, he never let on. I tried to act interested and enthusiastic about his ideas for places he wanted to go, like the Indian ruins at Puye Cliffs, the new recipes and restaurants he wanted to test, the musuems and movies he wanted to see.

He had the film developed of the wildflowers and the racetrack, and we spread the prints on the kitchen table. Some of the flowers were a little out of focus, but some were sharp as any picture in a book, the colors bright and clear. Among the scenes at the track, the jockeys in their brilliant silks and the sleek horses, was one very dark picture. At first I didn't recognize it. Then I made out Vinny Baca, standing in line at the betting window.

"Is that someone you know?" Elliott asked.

"I thought I did," I said, "but I guess I don't."

"It's considerably underexposed," Elliott said clinically. "I believe we discussed that at the time."

"Yes." I put it at the bottom of the pile.

"I need some portraits," he said, "photographs of me that can be used in reports and resumés. I want you to take them. These pictures show me you have a good eye."

That made me feel good. "When are you going to do it?"

"On our camping trip," he said. He waved at the pictures laid out on the table. "You can have any of those you want."

I picked out the field of Rocky Mountain iris, some of the wildflower close-ups, one of a jockey and his horse straining at the starting gate, and the dark shot of Vinny.

When I snapped that picture I had had some vague idea of showing it to Paul the next time he got mouthy and made some smart remark about Elliott. I planned to say something like, "Here's proof your amigo isn't the great guy you think he is. He's a compulsive gambler, he can't stay away from the ponies, and his wife is going to leave him if he doesn't quit." I was not going to do that now. Paul sure didn't need to have any more illusions destroyed. At home I destroyed the picture.

I met Paul accidentally one afternoon at K-Mart, the first I had seen him since he told me the story of his father. "Did you know the blockhouse was bull-dozed?" he asked. "They're bringing in the backhoe to start working on the new condos. Do you want to go watch?"

I didn't. I didn't think he wanted me to go either. Too much had been said, and we were both uncomfortable.

\* \* \*

We were going camping in Santa Clara Canyon. Paul's warning about Elliott and camping trips came back to me, and I realized I didn't care. Even if Elliott turned out to be what Paul said he was, that had nothing to do with me.

We would leave early Monday morning to avoid weekend crowds. By early, Elliott meant around six a.m. We'd set up the camp and go over to the cliffs before it got too hot. We'd be back in the canyon around noon and do whatever it was you did when you're camping. I had never been camping before, and I didn't know.

I told Ma the plans.

"That's good," she said.

Ma was still off somewhere in a hazy state, waiting for Hal to come back from Minnesota without Joey. If she married Hal, I'd have to get used to him being around all the time and Joey in the summers.

"I won't be here to babysit Donny."

"That's okay. I'll figure something out. I think you need to get out and have some fun. You've been real mopey."

"Can I borrow your daypack?"

"Sure."

Elliott was taking care of all the equipment, but he thought I should have some responsibility too. "You're in charge of lunch," he said. "I'll bring the rest of the food."

Another trip to the supermarket. I had managed to change some of the eating habits in our family. Ma said it was okay with her, I could get whatever I wanted, as long as it wasn't too expensive. So I generally bought big chunks of cheese and lots of eggs and even fresh vegetables, like spaghetti squash which I made into a casserole. I thought it was great, but Donny wouldn't touch it. Mrs. Montoya across the street kept us supplied with a steady harvest of vegetables from her garden. She thought it was funny that I was learning to cook, and she promised to show me how to roast green chilis for enchiladas and burritos and other New Mexican food.

I wasn't buying hotdogs and canned beans or canned ravioli. Hardly anything in cans. The one thing I could not get away from was marshmallow fluff. Donny threatened to run away from home if I didn't buy that, so I gave in.

Sunday afternoon I decided to bake bread for the picnic sandwiches as a surprise for Elliott. I kneaded it like crazy, thinking about Heather. She would have liked to bake bread, but we never got to do that. Maybe, if she wrote to me, I'd write back and explain how to do it. I planned to send her the Alfred E. Newman caricature too, so she'd remember me. But I guess I knew I'd never hear from her again.

While the dough was rising, I fixed a meatloaf, using Elliott's special recipe with salsa and cheese. I'd make sandwiches with it and leave the rest for Ma. Donny probably wouldn't touch it. I could not believe what a picky eater he was.

We'd have trail mix for dessert, with nuts and raisins and chopped-up fruit, like dried apricots, and M&Ms that wouldn't melt and get messy.

Very early the next morning I put the lunch in a paper bag, stuffed some clothes in Ma's daypack, and went out on the steps to wait. Hal's Saab was parked in front of the house. He was back from Minnesota. I hoped Elliott wouldn't ask about it.

At exactly six he drove up in the Land Cruiser.

"All set?" he asked.

"Let's go," I said and jumped in.

# TWENTY-FOUR

# CROSSING TO
# THE OTHER SIDE

A LITTLE STREAM notched a long, narrow canyon between two high ridges, crowded with ponderosas and spruce trees. It was long after sunup when we arrived, but the ridges rose so high that the canyon was in shadow. It was very still.

If you followed the dirt road all the way up through the canyon, Elliott said, you came to a series of ponds stocked with fish. Local people called them "lakes," but Elliott said they were not lakes by his definition.

We passed a few places where people had parked their RVs. "I hate those things," he said scornfully. "People drive them into these beautiful wilderness areas, and the first thing you know they've run up a television antenna and arranged a couple of lawn chairs in front, and they're cooking TV dinners in their microwave. You wonder why they ever left home."

This was not a civilized camping area with running water and flush toilets, he warned—just a couple of ramshackle latrines and a pump with drinking water further up the road. "All anybody needs," he said.

Elliott knew exactly where he was going. He pulled the Land Cruiser onto a broad flat place next to the stream. There was thick grass, big trees, the smell of pine, and the sound of rushing water. A log crossed to the base of the steep hillside. Elliott said the huge trees were Engelmann spruce, identifiable by clusters of cones near the top.

"What d'you think?" Elliott asked, waving at the site he had chosen.

"I like it."

A grassy bank sloped down to the stream that gurgled and sang on its way to wherever it was going. There had been a huge snowpack in the area in the winter, and although now, toward the end of summer, the stream should have been down to a trickle, it was still strong. I stooped down to look at the sandy bottom through the clear water and watched a couple of leaves sweep out of sight.

"Hey!" Elliott yelled. "Think you're on vacation?"

We went over the area thoroughly, deciding on the perfect location for the tent. Elliott said he preferred to sleep outside, but a tent was a good idea in case of a sudden storm. And bears. There were known to be bears in the canyon.

We found exactly the right spot on a layer of pine needles and spread the groundcloth. Elliott dug a little trough around it with a trenching tool so that any possible rain water didn't end up inside. He showed me how to erect the dome tent with a bunch of thin nylon rods that snapped together and slid through a series of cloth tubes in an ingenious way. Eventually it began to make sense, and I got it put together and anchored to pegs in case a wind blew up.

There was a wooden picnic table near the tent and a blackened stone fireplace. Elliott unpacked the breakfast things and in a few minutes had a pot of coffee perking on the Coleman stove.

"I've been camping with that old pot for thirty-five years," he said.

He boiled water to fix hot chocolate for me—it was chilly here in the canyon, without the sun on us yet—and then to make oatmeal. He cut up an apple and added raisins and cinnamon and poured real cream over it, and even though I believed I didn't like oatmeal, this was delicious.

Elliott settled down under a tree with a mug of coffee, the picture of a happy man. I was feeling a lot better, too, but that ended when he spied the log over the stream. I watched him balance across, carrying the coffee mug. He stopped in the middle to watch the water rush by a foot or so beneath him.

"Looks like a trail running up the side of the ridge from here. Let's see where it goes."

"No thanks," I said.

He turned back and looked at me. "You really don't want to investigate?"

How could I tell him I was scared of crossing logs? I found that out when Ma and Donny and Joe Favello and I went on a picnic a long time ago, and they all walked across, even Donny, who was just a little kid, and I stood there paralyzed. Joe coaxed and then insisted and finally got mad and yelled and made fun of me and said I was a coward, until Ma told him to shut up and leave me alone. They went on without me.

I knew I wasn't going to cross this one either. I don't know what there was about it that made it so scary, because it wasn't even that far above the water and if I fell in, so what? But still I couldn't move. Ma said I had a phobia about it.

"You go ahead," I told Elliott. "That's okay."

He came back and sat down at the wooden table across from me. "Are you all right, Win?"

"Sort of."

" 'Sort of.' Now what does that mean, exactly?"

"It means everything's been going bad lately and I can't do anything right."

"You want to tell me about it?"

I shook my head.

Elliott sat quietly for a while, sipping his coffee, which was probably stone cold by then.

"Why don't you want to go for a walk on the other side of the stream?"

"I thought we were going to the cliff dwellings," I said. "I thought you were in such a hurry to do that, that's why we came out here while it was still practically dark."

"Is that the only reason? You think I'm in such a hurry to get to the cliffs? Or are you in such a hurry?"

"I'm not in any hurry. I don't care if we go to the cliffs at all!"

"I think you'll enjoy them, but maybe we ought

to let that go and hang around the camp this morning. Go for a walk, get oriented. Up that trail on the other side of the creek, for instance."

"No thanks!"

Elliott picked up my mug and mixed some more hot chocolate and refilled his own mug with coffee. "I'm not going to ask you to tell me anything you don't want to, because I respect your privacy and it's none of my business. But I wish you'd tell me what you've got against the other side of that stream."

I chased a couple of bugs along a crack in the wooden table. "I'm scared to cross logs," I mumbled.

"Ah, so that's it," he said. "Remember a talk we had a long time ago about fear? It's possible to overcome fear. I don't think I ever told you I used to be afraid of heights. I couldn't go up a ladder. I was scared to climb a tree. Then one summer in high school I got a job working for a landscaper, the only job I could find, and he wanted me to climb a big maple and take out some dead branches. I was petrified, but he helped me get over it. We did it one branch at a time. He was patient with me, because he said he had once been afraid of heights too. He climbed up to a branch about six feet off the ground, and I climbed up and sat with him. Then after a while he moved to a higher branch and sat there for a while. The next day we did it again and went a little higher. After a while I got over it. Now it doesn't bother me at all. I take that back: it hardly ever bothers me."

"That would work with logs too, I guess."

"If you want it to."

"How would I do it?"

"I suggest first of all that we forget Puye Cliffs for now. We can do that later. Agreed?"

"Okay."

"We'll look around here and see if we can't find a great thick log that crosses a very narrow stream, that's maybe even lying in the stream. Did you bring any other shoes?"

"No."

"If you had, I'd suggest you jump off the log into the water, just to see that even if you do fall in, it's okay. But never mind that. Let's just go look for a twelve-inch log lying about four inches above the water."

We found one, Elliott walked out to the middle of it, and I walked after him. There was nothing to that. He had me stand there for a while, to get used to the idea of that moving water below me, and turn around, sit down, and stand up again, walk back and forth and back and forth. When we had just about worn out that log, we found another one.

This one was not as thick and it hung several inches higher above the water, but it was only a couple of steps across. Elliott repeated the lesson—walked partway across, had me follow him, and made me stop, sit down, stand up, turn around.

Slowly we worked our way up the dirt road, Elliott on the lookout for logs for me to practice on. Every now and then we'd have to step aside as a pickup tore by, churning up dust, men in baseball caps riding in the cab, kids sitting back in the bed with fishing poles. Elliott always waved, and sometimes they waved back.

The little stream wandered first on one side of the

road, then the other, channelled beneath the road through the pipes big enough to crawl through. Hawks floated in the blue sky, and Elliott said he had heard there were a couple of golden eagles in the area. The sun had climbed over the sharp edge of the ridge, and the valley was bright and hot.

Elliott always managed to find a log a little tougher, a little more challenging, than the last one. He'd walk across, checking the difficulty. Then he'd come back and we'd study it.

"Keep going once you get started. Look to see where you're putting your feet but don't stop and look down at the water. Keep up your momentum."

We'd shake hands. "Good luck," he'd say. "See you on the other side." And he'd walk across the log, turn around, and face me. I'd lock my eyes with his for a second, take a deep breath, and go. We'd shake hands again, and he'd say, "Congratulations. Well done." And I'd say, "Thank you."

The sun was high overhead when we dawdled back to our campsite. "I'm surprised that you haven't been howling for food," he said. "It's been several hours since breakfast."

I had been too worried about the next log to think about eating. "Remember I brought the lunch," I said.

"Right. But before you break it out, let's have a final examination. Let's see you walk across that log now."

It was a long log, not more than six inches thick, angled across the creek. Elliott sat down at the picnic table and waited, and I climbed up on the end of the log. Suddenly out of nowhere a thought of Heather

came back to me, her iris-colored eyes wide with terror.
I panicked and froze. I don't know how long I stood
there until Elliott came and led me back to the table.

"Too much for one day," he said. "You'll be able
to handle that one tomorrow."

But I was thinking of Heather and doubted that I
ever could.

There wasn't much to say. I got our sandwiches
out of the ice chest. Elliott commented on the meat
loaf and the homemade bread and praised me for my
good cooking. Wonderful, I thought: Win Kelly, the
Cowardly Cook, the All-American Ass. A terror in the
kitchen, but don't ask him to do anything that requires
any guts, except eating. He's real good at that.

"We could use some more drinking water," Elliott
said when we had finished lunch. "Want to take a walk
up the road to the pump?"

"I'll get it," I said. I needed to be off by myself for
a little while. Elliott seemed to understand. He unpacked a book, settled under a tree, and put on his half
glasses. "I'll be right here," he said.

I swung off up the dusty road with the plastic jug.
It was very hot now. Butterflies flitted around, but that
seemed to be the only thing moving in the noonday
heat. When I passed some of the logs I had been practicing on with Elliott in the morning, I looked the
other way.

I was in no hurry. I didn't want to rush back to
the campsite where Elliott might want to talk, so I kept
on going past the pump toward the fishing ponds. Then
I noticed that it wasn't quite so hot. A fluffy cloud
passed over the sun briefly, and then another. Soon a

whole drift of clouds had ganged up over the ridge and settled there, looking dark and heavy.

I trotted back to the pump and splashed water into the jug. Filled with a couple of gallons, it was much heavier, and it banged awkwardly against my leg as I hurried back to camp. It was further than I thought.

The first cold raindrops slapped against my face. I tried to jog, but it was slow going, and the drops fell harder and faster. Then I saw Elliott trotting up the road toward me. We made a dash for the tent together and dived inside, soaked and gasping.

I peeled off my wet clothes and put on dry ones and stretched out on the sleeping bag Elliott was lending me. He had already brought in the stash of trail mix and a portable chess set. This wasn't beautiful like the ceramic chess set we had used the first time, but it was much handier. A little peg on the bottom of each plastic piece fit into a tiny hole in the square, so you could play on the deck of a rolling ship or in a high wind. Elliott still won, but it was taking him longer to beat me.

The rain drummed on the tent, which was bathed in a pale greenish light. Elliott asked if I had brought anything along to read. Since I hadn't thought of that, he said I could read one of his books, a collection of short stories by Ernest Hemingway.

Elliott said Hemingway used to go big game hunting in Africa back in the days when people went on safaris to shoot elephants and lions. They don't do that any more; now vanloads of tourists drive around with their cameras, and the only trophy they get is a photograph. I started to read the first story, "The Short

Happy Life of Francis Macomber," about a guy who was a coward. I felt sorry for Francis Macomber, trying to stalk a wounded lion and scared to death, ashamed in front of his wife and the guide. I knew exactly how he felt.

After a while the rain stopped and the sun came out long enough to dry things off before it slid down behind the western ridge of the canyon. I crawled out of the tent into the clean, fresh-smelling air and went down to the stream to watch some more leaves swirl by.

Elliott followed me. "Let's go to the cliffs," he said.

"Now? Isn't it too late?"

"Now."

# TWENTY-FIVE
## ELLIOTT & WIN

A LADDER made of poles leaned against the face of the cliff. Elliott climbed first, me right below him, up to the little caves hollowed in the soft stone. It must have been a big city at one time; the cliff was like a honeycomb. Now it was deserted. The Indians had left it long ago, and the tourists had all gone home.

"These tribes drifted down from Colorado almost fifteen hundred years ago," Elliott explained. "See the rows of small holes above the caves? They built rooms out from the cliffs, and those holes held the supporting beams."

We crept along a narrow path and crawled in and out of the small caves, Elliott hunched over almost double. The Indians who lived there must have been very short. I crouched in one of the caves and tried to imagine what life had been like there.

A narrow stairway cut in the rock led to the top of the mesa. The Indians who left the caves and moved up there had built their homes of stone. Most of the buildings had collapsed, and only the low outlines remained. Inside the ruined walls tall grass grew, bent over by the wind that swept steadily across the mesa.

"Amazing builders, weren't they?" Elliott said admiringly.

Elliott had brought his camera; this was where he wanted me to take his picture, a gray-bearded chief posed against the ruins of the ancient city. He handed me the camera and let me take a few close-ups and full-length shots without once telling me how to set it. "Take some others, if you want to," he said, but I shook my head and handed it back.

How did it feel to grow up in a place like that, among people like that, at that time? If I had been a boy here I would have helped to grow squash, corn, beans, and cotton. I looked out over the green trees dotting the pink earth and realized how far I would have had to hike to get water, climbing back up here with an earthen jar on my shoulders. I would have hunted with my father for deer and turkey and maybe even bear. Must have been hard being an Indian, but at least you knew what you were supposed to be, what you were expected to do. You were taught to be brave, and your manhood was tested in various ways. I probably couldn't have passed the test.

We came to the kiva, the underground ceremonial place, and climbed down another pole ladder through a small opening into the large circular room. The floor was dirt, the wall lined with stone, and the ceiling made of saplings laid close together over log beams. Elliott sat down near the ladder on a stone bench that circled the room. Sunlight poured through the opening, focused like a spotlight. I moved into the shadows.

"When this was in use," Elliott said, "there was a firepit in the center, and somewhere in the floor was an opening, the entrance to the spirit world, the place through which life came into this world. It does feel like a womb, doesn't it?"

He climbed up the ladder. "Stay as long as you like," he said. "I'm going to take some pictures of walls."

The darkness and the rough stones reminded me too much of the blockhouse, and the terrible scene went through my mind one more time like a bad movie. I felt choked, as though my wind was being shut off. I rushed for the ladder.

Dinner showed all the signs of being an Elliott Deerfield production. He sent me out to scrounge some wood for the campfire we'd have later. When I came back from foraging with a sack of twigs and a few dead branches, Elliott had backed the Land Cruiser around to get at his built-in pantry and had converted one end of the picnic table into a work area. The other end was set with a tablecloth, silverware, glasses, and plates.

"Time to wean you away from soda pop," Elliott said, pouring something bubbly and colorless. "That is Perrier, and here's a slice of lime. Sip on that while I cook."

Out of the cooler came a pair of chicken breasts that he pounded thin, between pieces of waxed paper, with a rock. He put little red new potatoes on to boil and handed me a couple of ears of corn to shuck. A pan with melted butter was ready for the chicken.

"Fresh from the garden," he said, slicing a giant tomato. He had a tiny garden next to the patio with four tomato plants and a couple of zucchinis that he fussed over. The tomatoes were a trade-off for the corn, which I knew he got for me even though he didn't like it much. He said corn on the cob wasn't particularly nutritious, and it stuck in his teeth. To please him I would eat his tomatoes.

Elliott opened a bottle of white wine, explained what kind it was, what variety of grapes were used to make it, what vineyard they had come from, what year it was bottled, how this particular type was different from some other, and so on. I used to think anybody who cared about all that must be crazy, but I had learned over the summer that Elliott wasn't crazy. Unusual, yes. Individual, yes. Crazy, no.

The light was fading in our narrow valley. Elliott hung a lantern on a tree limb and set a pair of candles in glass globes on the table, creating an island of yellow light. The sound of the stream seemed louder now, and an owl hooted softly nearby. The chicken sizzled in the butter and smelled wonderful. I was thinking how I'd describe all this in *The Adventures of Elliott and Win.*

It was a terrific meal, not at all what you think of when you think of camping. We ate real slow, because there wouldn't be much to do after we finished. The chess set might come out again, or we could read by lantern light. But there was always a surprise with Elliott. He pulled a little tin pipe from his pack and played a tune on it.

"It's a penny whistle," he said, "given me by an Irishman in a Dublin pub. The Irishman, Todd Casey was his name, played it and everyone sang along. That's one of the gifts of the Irish, in addition to being wonderful storytellers. The only time I blow it is out camping, so forgive me if I'm a bit rusty."

He handed it to me and let me toot on it while he built a fire in the circle of stones. When it was crackling he tried to explain how the fingering went on the pipe, but I was a hopeless pupil and gave it back.

Elliott played a lot of songs I didn't know, "old favorites" he called them. I don't know whose favorites they were. Not mine, but they were pretty.

One had such a sad, sweet tone that it made *me* sad, and I didn't know what I was going to do with all that sadness welling up inside me. Tears began leaking down my face. I brushed them away and turned my head so Elliott wouldn't notice.

About the sixth time he caught me scrubbing at my cheeks, he put down the pennywhistle. "Win, I know something's wrong," he said. "Do you want to talk about it?"

I shook my head. "I don't know what to say."

"I don't either."

We were both quiet for a while, and then he tried again. "I'm not sure I can help you with anything, but I can listen. Sometimes if you just talk about what's bothering you, you feel better."

"I know," I said, even though I didn't. "I'm scared to start talking because I'm afraid once I start I can't stop." I tried to laugh, but it came out weird.

"We've got plenty of time." He picked up his pennywhistle and started playing again, real soft and sad, and pretty soon the tears were dribbling. He came around and stood behind me and laid his hands on my shoulders, very lightly. I started to sob like a broken-hearted little baby, but somehow I didn't feel embarrassed.

"Is it something with your mother?"

I swallowed hard. "That's part of it." I told him about Hal Norris being Donny's new amigo and Ma's new boyfriend, and if Ma was falling in love with him our lives would change one more time.

Talking got easier. Elliott stayed close behind me so I could feel his warmth, but I didn't have to look at him.

I told him about Heather.

I hadn't said much about Heather before. Conversations with Elliott tended to be about things, not about people. I explained how we got to be friends, beginning when she came to the yard sale and bought his old magazines.

"She said she wanted to drop out of school because the kids made so much fun of her, because she had such big, uh, you know, breasts. Even the girls were nasty. I tried to tell her it was no worse than having freckles, but she didn't believe me, and I know now she was right."

"What happened?"

I told the story then, of the picnic and the block-house and the guys who came there. Elliott didn't say anything while I struggled through the story. He didn't move. The hands stayed on my shoulders, steady and warm, until I had finished. Then he sat down beside me.

"Where's Heather now?"

"She and her mother are on their way to San Francisco. They've probably already left. Her father stayed to sell the cookie shop, and then he's going too."

"Have you seen her since that night?"

"Her mom wouldn't let me. She said Heather was too upset. But then I saw her a few days ago at the library, and she told me she was leaving." I started to bawl again. "It was my fault, Elliott!"

"What makes you think it was your fault?"

"I should never have taken her to the blockhouse. Ma always told me something bad would happen there, that drug dealers and bums probably hung out there at night, but I had been there lots of times in the daytime with Paul and never saw nobody—*anybody*—around."

"That doesn't make it your fault, Win. You made an error of judgment, that's all. There's a big difference."

"Yeah, but don't you see? I couldn't protect her. I couldn't do one thing to help her!"

"There were how many? Four fellows? How could you possibly have protected her?"

"If I had had a gun—"

"You want to start carrying a gun around with you? That's not the answer."

I was sobbing then, remembering how scared and helpless I felt. I could not get the picture out of my head, of Heather on the floor of the blockhouse, of the look in her eyes. "I'll see her face until I die," I said.

"I think," Elliott said slowly, "you need to talk to somebody."

"I'm talking to you," I snuffled.

"To a professional counselor. Somebody who can help you understand that it wasn't your fault. Maybe you ought to talk to Dr. Sara Vogel. She's a psychologist, remember. I'll bet she'd help you get rid of the picture in your mind."

"I don't want to talk about it," I said. "I just want it to go away."

"The problem is that bad pictures don't simply go away. You might be able to squeeze it into some dark corner so that you hardly notice it, but it's still there, liable to pop out when you least expect it. Better to do the hard thing and deal with it now, instead of pretending it doesn't exist."

"Maybe."

"I've got another idea, though. I want you to know that this will not happen to you again. Watch."

He kicked off his shoes and placed the candles on the ground. Then he began to execute the movements of a *kata*.

"This is the bear," he said, performing some bear-like moves. "This is the tiger . . . this is the mongoose . . . this is the white crane. . . ."

He finished the *kata* with the cobra and the dragon and bowed formally to me.

"You and I are going to see Jack Mooney about kung fu lessons. Once you get your *chi* flowing, you'll be able to handle four attackers with no trouble at all."

Night had settled into the canyon. We got ready for bed and crawled into our sleeping bags. Elliott blew out the lantern. "Good night, Win," he said, and in about thirty seconds his breathing was slow and deep.

It took me a while to get comfortable. A couple of pickups rattled by, their headlights sweeping through the darkness and glowing briefly in our tent. I lay there and listened to an owl calling and the water hurrying on its way to somewhere.

In the darkness I saw myself executing the moves of the bear, the tiger, the mongoose, the crane. I was powerful and sure. Four dark men with evil, gleaming eyes dropped helplessly at my feet. Heather's iris-colored eyes glowed at me with trust and love.

As I drifted off to sleep, my best friend began to snore.